1,000-YEAR VOYAGE

1,000-YEAR VOYAGE

JOHN RUSSELL FEARN

WILDSIDE PRESS

To the Memory of Florence Rose Fearn

CONTENTS

CHAPTER ONE

BANISHMENT

THERE had come a time in the affairs of men when absolute dictatorship was not only being questioned, but completely destroyed. The people of Earth were no longer inclined to accept one man and his retinue of chosen adherents as the deciders of their habits, actions, and future. As a direct consequence of this there had been revolution—not the ruthless massacre of bombs and blood—but the insidious inroads of clever politics, which, by vote alone had deposed the Dictator and his retinue from absolute power, and instead placed them at the mercy of the Supreme Court of Earth.

This master of the Earth who had gained such absolute control was known as Rigilus I. By the dual use of politics and resort to arms be had not only conquered the World but had gained the complete mastery of every colonized body in the Solar System.... At least for a time. Now had come the inversion of policy with Rigilus I called to account.

Not that he looked particularly troubled on this summer morning in the twenty-third century, as with the dozen men and women who had been his loyal supporters he sat in the Box of the Accused and surveyed the grim faces of his persecutors with a complete and proud arrogance. Rigilus the First looked and had been every inch a ruler. There was no sentiment in that ruggedly cut face; very little sign of the more delicate of human feelings in that harshly chiselled mouth. Here was a man born to dominate, and dominate he had until his decrees had gone beyond what the peoples of the Earth and the Solar System considered reasonable. Now there was a People's Government intent on only one thing—the dispensation of just punishment for the twenty odd years of power which Rigilus I had maintained.

"For such as you," said the People's Prosecutor, from his position high up in the mighty amphitheatre, "Nothing less than complete banishment will suffice. Your high position and that of those who have been gathered about you make it necessary that you should be granted a certain amount of clemency and for that reason the ultimate sentence of Death is not passed upon you. We feel, after due deliberation among ourselves, that banishment is quite the most fitting punishment that can be meted out to such as you. You who love power and authority and the control of helpless millions will be utterly subjected if forced to lead the rest of your life in comparative solitude, unable to dominate, isolated completely from those worlds which you have ruled so long.

"For the effectual implication of your sentence, therefore, we have decided that you shall be banished to the Deeps of Outer Space in the region of the nearest Star—Alpha Centauri. You are being sent, Rigilus I, on a journey which, for you at least, there can be no end. Alpha Centauri being so far away that you cannot possibly reach it in your lifetime, or indeed in a dozen lifetimes. Have you anything to say as to why this sentence should not be passed upon you?"

Rigilus rose to his feet, an insolently erect figure. With proud disdain he surveyed the faces all turned in his direction.

"I have only this to say," he said, quietly, "that the banishment of my colleagues and myself to the distant regions of Alpha Centauri only means the ridding of Earth of myself and the sect in which I believe for something like fifteen generations. For believe me the power of Rigilus I will not be broken merely by banishing me to Alpha Centauri. Others will come after me, my sons and daughters and their sons and daughters, all of whom will be educated to believe that this monstrous injustice must one day be avenged.

"Putting it more briefly there will come a time, maybe fifteen, twenty, or maybe thirty generations hence, when the sentence you have passed here this day will recoil upon you, or at least your descendants, with such shattering effect that those who follow you will bemoan the fact that you ever dared to tear down the dictatorship of myself and my colleagues. Speaking less personally, I find it difficult to conceive what you find so wrong about me and those that have been so loyal to me. We have served you well, we have given you every amenity, we have built up science to a supreme peak and given you a civilisation of which you can be justifiably proud.

"Add to this the fact that every colonised body in the Solar System from our Moon to the largest moon of Saturn has been brought under our aegis, and yet you are still not satisfied and must tear down the mind and the hands that conceived it. Why? At least, I am surely entitled to know that."

Upon which Rigilus sat down again and his comrades around him nodded in silent confirmation.

The People's Prosecutor looked about him and cleared his throat. It was obvious that for the moment he did not quite know what he ought to reply, and the sardonic smile being directed towards him from Rigilus did not altogether help matters, either.

"Our reason for deposing you," he said at length, "is one that should be more or less evident to you. You have, in the course of your many years of office, paid little heed to the individual desires of the men and women you controlled, with the result that they have become little better than robots. Any attempt at them exerting an individuality of their own has been ruthlessly snuffed out, and whatever progress we have made has been entirely the work of yourself or those immediately under you. For that reason, that men and women may regain their own initiative before it is too late, we have felt it necessary to remove from you the absolute power that you have wielded. There is nothing more that can be said, Rigilus I. We are decided what shall be done, and the details relevant to your banishment are given you herewith...."

There was a rustle of paper as the Prosecutor went through his notes, then after considering them carefully he looked up again and across the vast space where Rigilus sat waiting in stony calm.

For Rigilus this whole thing was vastly disturbing. Much that the Prosecutor had said had been nothing else but lies—or if not that, a trumped-up story. No man could have done more in the past twenty years than Rigilus for the advancement of science and the comfort of the human race in general. The main reason for his deposition had not been because of the ruthless nature of his edicts, but because of that jealous strain in human nature that refuses to give credit to anything cleverer than itself. For that reason and none other, Rigilus and his comrades were now faced with the ultimate punishment—banishment.

"It has been decided," the People's Prosecutor continued after a moment or two, "that you will have placed at your disposal one of our largest space machines. As far as accommodation is concerned it equals the size of any small city, and has therein every amenity one would expect to find in such a city. This, together with all the necessary synthesising apparatus for the making of foods, clothes and other essentials should prove entirely suitable for your practically endless voyage. You will be permitted to take with you whomever you choose from amongst your own retinue, but nobody else. Since your retinue is composed of men and women, all of them married, you will perceive therein a certain clemency in our sense of justice. In other words, there can be future generations to carry on the colossal voyage that you will start, and which, providing you make the entire trip without any cosmic disaster, will take you 1,000 years! There is surely nothing in that, Rigilus, with which you can find fault?"

"One thousand years seems an absurdly long time," Rigilus commented. "Surely if our ship was to maintain a constant acceleration, it could in time build its speed up to an appreciable fraction of that of light itself? With such a velocity that time could be vastly reduced, even allowing for deceleration at the other end."

"*If* is the operative word," replied the People's Prosecutor, with a certain acid satisfaction. "However, the acceleration will *not* be constant! It will build up to a certain speed, and when that speed is reached, the atomic engine will be switched off. Thereafter your vessel will coast in free space at a constant velocity, until you near your destination. The controls are mathematically pre-set to carry you through the void straight to the region of Alpha Centauri. The distance and the time taken to cover that distance—one thousand years—has been mathematically calculated and linked by an electronic brain to the controls. That means that the controls will only become free when you are within measurable distance of the Alpha Centauri System. That is something that you will have to teach your successors, for the time will inevitably come when they will be compelled to understand the controlling of the vessel if they are to make a safe landing and not crash upon some infinitely distant world. The main thing that we are concerned about is that you never return."

Rigilus digested this shattering information for a moment or two, then gave a shrug. "I can only repeat what I said earlier, namely—

that the day will come when you will deeply regret the dispensation of sentence now accorded to me. Since my colleagues are completely allied to me there can be no doubt that I am also expressing their sentiments."

Rigilus looked round upon his immediate retinue and they nodded their heads in silent assent, High up on his seat of office the People's Prosecutor looked somewhat relieved that he had managed to hurdle this most difficult of all situations. In himself he did not entirely agree either with the sentence or with the deposition of Rigilus, but he was in the unfortunate position of having to do exactly as he was told.

"There is nothing further then to be said," the People's Prosecutor commented after a while. "The decision has been taken and nothing remains but for it to be carried out. For the time being, Rigilus, you and your colleagues will be under what is technically known as House-arrest—insofar as you will be confined to your particular dwellings under close guard—and at midnight tomorrow you will assemble aboard the space liner which will carry you to your destination unknown."

"Just one more thing," Rigilus said, rising to his feet again. "Have I your permission to ask a question of the First in Astronomy?"

"Permission granted," the Prosecutor assented.

Rigilus turned and looked towards the man who was acknowledged to be the leading authority on astronomical subjects throughout the world.

"Of late years," Rigilus said, "I have not found it possible to conduct a very thorough study of astronomy—having left all of it to the experts in that particular field. But it now becomes essential that I know of certain facts before I am launched out into the void along with my colleagues. I am, of course, an expert in the control of a space machine, but my knowledge of the void is limited to the Solar System. What lies beyond I do not know. I therefore call upon you, the First in Astronomy, to tell me whether at the end of this colossal 1,000-year voyage, there is likely to be any goal that we may seek— any resting place where we may at last cease our eternal vigil in the void. Or, at least, that our successors might find?"

The First in Astronomy did not hesitate over giving his reply.

"According to our close examination of the spatial regions around Alpha Centauri and Proxima Centauri, there does exist the possibility of a planetary system and even the added possibility of worlds not unlike Earth. By that, I mean that their atmospheres and general gravity correspond fairly closely to that of this world. It should be possible for you to locate one of those worlds and land upon it. What you do after that is no concern of ours—indeed it can never be since 1,000 years hence we who are here today will no longer be concerned with the situation."

"Thank you," Rigilus responded, with regal calm. "And now, People's Prosecutor, one other question. Are we to be allowed absolute freedom in the space machine which has been assigned to us?"

"Certainly, but there is the one proviso I have already mentioned. You can have all the liberty that you require and may mould your lives exactly as you wish, but you will never be able to interfere with the controls of the space machine itself. By that I mean that you will not be able to guide it in any way, to perhaps return in due course to wreak this vengeance that you speak of."

"In the course of years, and with very little else to do," Rigilus said, slowly, "there will be nothing to prevent us taking the electronic brain to pieces and thereby gaining control of the space machine to do with as we will. Had you, in your supreme wisdom, considered that possibility?"

"Definitely we had," the Prosecutor replied, "and for that reason we have taken special precautions. Each part of the electronic brain is so designed that if any part of it is removed, that part will inevitably be destroyed. The design is such that there are no machine-instruments aboard the vessel for you to make a fresh piece, therefore, any tampering with the electronic brain will mean that you automatically destroy it.

"Further, if you do destroy the electronic brain the ship will be completely out of control and consequently at the mercy of any meteorites or foreign bodies there may be in space. Also it would make it impossible for you to make a landing upon another planet. You would simply crash and that would be the end. From all of this you will have gathered that tampering with the electronic brain is not to be recommended."

Rigilus said no more. Everything had evidently been thought out well in advance and there was nothing that he and his colleagues could do to alter the situation....

Just how completely everything had been planned they realised the following night at midnight, when they were conducted aboard the space liner. It was one of the biggest and latest machines in the huge Earth-Space Travel Combine, and, as the People's Prosecutor had said, was supplied with every possible necessity for an indefinite journey. Entering its airlock, Rigilus and his colleagues found themselves within a tremendous control room from which led the main passageway off which again were the doors of the ship's various departments. The space machine was indeed a travelling city within itself, and containing everything that the banished travellers could possibly need.

Present at the departure ceremony were the People's Prosecutor and the small gathering who had formed themselves into the Government that had deposed Rigilus himself. They now stood in the great control room face to face with the ex-ruler and his colleagues, their animosity typified by the cold barrier that had fallen between them.

"I have executed my duty as I was directed to do," the People's Prosecutor said, briefly, merely mouthing the words of the legal formula usually meted out to banished travellers, "and thereby, my responsibility ends. You know exactly where your destination will be and no power of yours will alter it. Should you die on the way the ship will continue its journey carrying corpses. And may the Cosmos have mercy upon you...."

Such was the brief, formal ceremony, and then the People's Prosecutor turned and stepped back through the airlock, followed by his colleagues. Rigilus watched them go, a grave smile on his ruggedly-hewn face. He glanced at his comrades for a moment, then turned and crossed to the switchboard moving the lever that quickly closed the immense airlock. The moment the sound of the bolts gliding into place had ceased Rigilus turned and looked about him.

"Upon the injustice of this situation there is very little comment that we can make," he said, quietly. "The only thing that we can do is make the best of it, and being intelligent men and women, fully gifted with the knowledge of scientific resources we will certainly do that. We are not even burdened with the piloting of the machine since it will pilot itself, so then, let us be on our way. There is just one thing that must be understood before we make our departure, and that is, that within this vessel *I* am still the ruler."

The others nodded but did not comment. For a reason that Rigilus did not quite comprehend they looked at each other momentarily as though they were exchanging confirmations of some hidden thought. In any case Rigilus was not particularly concerned with his colleagues at the moment, his main objective was to be free of the Earth and out in space where he would be able to plan more freely.

He glanced enquiringly at his comrades. Understanding exactly what he meant they crossed to the airbed racks set against the walls and one by one settled themselves down, buckling the straps across them. Rigilus waited until every one of them was securely bedded down, then he gave his slow, grave smile.

"This, my friends," he said, quietly, "is quite the most impressive moment in our career. We are abandoning the world of our birth and the Solar System itself, to enter upon a journey the end of which we shall never see. I want each of you to promise now—yes, even before we lift from the surface of the Earth—that you will inculcate into your children nothing but hatred for the world of Earth and the people who now rule it. This moment of monstrous injustice must be avenged no matter how long it takes and no matter how many generations have to be inoculated with the poison of revenge. Do I have promise from each one of you?"

All told there were eleven others besides Rigilus—five men and six women—and although none of them actually spoke each one of them nodded an assent. Rigilus could not help feeling that there was something very perfunctory about that acquiescence, but nevertheless he had to be satisfied with it. He turned to the switchboard, settled in the massive driving seat and then switched on the atomic power engines. Immediately their droning rhythm pervaded the enormous vessel.

As Rigilus well knew there was enough power in atomic form to carry the vessel not for one thousand years but for five thousand if need be, so if by some fluke there ever was a chance of turning back, even when the absolute limit of the journey had been made, the attempt would not be stillborn for lack of fuel.

Such was the final thought that passed through Rigilus' mind before he closed the contact that transferred the enormous potential of power into the rocket jets. The moment that happened the ship lifted with superlative ease, a creation of the finest engineering genius which Earth possessed—which was only another way of saying that Rigilus himself had been the original designer of modern space travel propulsion systems. Because of him space travel had been changed from the dangerous fuel-hungry rocketry that it had been in the beginning to a sublime journeying without any danger between one world and another. True there had been other engineers who had made modifications, but the basis of perfected space travel could always be ascribed to Rigilus I.

Swift as a bird for all its colossal weight, the space liner hurtled far above the master city of the world, the gravity nullifiers operating perfectly to counteract the tremendous drag of the acceleration. Efficient though they were they could not entirely negate that sense of smothering pressures which remained until the vessel was at last clear of the Earth's atmosphere and with every second was beginning to lose the counteracting pull of Earth's own mass.

Rigilus sat on at the controls glancing only occasionally at his supine colleagues. Thus he remained until at last the last traces of gravitational drag had disappeared and the vessel was sweeping onwards into space following the course that the now operative electronic brain had already devised for it. Once free of the Earth's pull, the ship continued to accelerate steadily, and this, combined with the activation of the gravity-plates under the deck, combined to give the effect of an Earth-normal gravity to the travellers.

Rigilus checked the instruments and then got up from his chair, moving thoughtfully into the centre of the control room. He stood there debating whilst his comrades released themselves from their airbeds. One by one they came across to him and there was something in their expressions that he could not quite understand, particularly in the faces of the women.

"Something is troubling you, my friends," he remarked, towering amongst them, "unfortunately we have plenty of time in which to debate whatever it might be. Perhaps you would care to tell me?"

"That is precisely our purpose. If you will be so good as to come into the lounge, Rigilus," one of the men responded, "we will make clear what is in our minds."

Rigilus gave a long, searching look, then with a shrug he complied leading the way down the long corridor into the enormous lounge through the window of which the great rim of the receding Earth loomed against the black void.

With his usual majestic movements Rigilus seated himself and then raised tufted eyebrows enquiringly. Like a debating society the men and women drew up chairs and settled themselves regarding him steadily. He could not escape the certain air of accusation that hung around.

"Rigilus," one of the men said, at length, looking at him steadily, "you know me well enough to understand that I am well entitled to speak for the others?"

"Well of course, Randos," Rigilus responded, smiling. "You have been my first in command for long enough. What is it that you wish to tell me?"

"Just this. We have been considering among ourselves the scheme of vengeance that you insist must be inculcated into whatever generations follow us. I am speaking for everybody here when I say that we are not in agreement with your suggestion."

"Since when," Rigilus asked calmly, "have you taken it upon yourselves to question my edicts? I have said what must be done, Randos, and done it shall be."

"Not in this instance. You are forgetting, Rigilus, that you are no longer master of the world and ourselves the members of your immediate clique. You are simply the commander of a space machine on a one thousand year journey. Or, to reduce things to a more common denominator, you are one of us! Ten of us are against your decision and no power that you possess can make us change it!"

"All else apart," Rigilus said, puzzled, "I'm quite at a loss to understand why you should be willing to bow to the so-called justice of Earth people and do absolutely nothing about it. Am I to understand that you consider the sentence passed upon us was entirely justified?"

"That," Randos replied, "is neither here nor there. For one thing we can never live to see the result of this scheme of vengeance and therefore it has little or no attraction for us. You have only one supporter in your desire for revenge, Rigilus, and that is Merva Ansof."

Randos nodded towards her, a slim, dark, intensely sophisticated woman, one who had been Rigilus' right hand through the latter years of his Earthly campaign. She was still only young, but as cool, efficient, and as ruthless as an electronic brain itself.

"At least," Rigilus remarked, glancing towards her and giving a slight inclination of his head, "it is pleasant to know that I have one supporter."

"Two against ten," Randos pointed out. "All the rest of us here are married couples, only you and Merva Ansof are not married. Obviously if the far flung destination of the Alpha Centauri is ever to be reached we must have children, and they in turn must have their children and so on and so on generation after generation until there finally comes that generation which will end the voyage. *But* we none of us propose to bring into this space machine children who will be brought up on nothing else but the gospel of vengeance.

"We prefer to look upon what has happened to us as something which is entirely connected with *our* generation and with that, let it die. Let our children's children find a world on which to start again and not be clouded with the knowledge that they must return across this awful waste of space to deal with the successors of those who banished us."

Rigilus mused, his massive face thrown half into shadow by the brilliance of sunlight on one side and the pale orange glow of the ceiling lights on the other. Merva Ansof stirred very slightly, her cold green eyes surveying the rest of the assembly with a shattering contempt.

"Fools, all of you," she said at length, in her low contralto voice. "You are content to let these idiots of Earth do what they will to us and not exact any payment for it? I would be prepared to have children—yes, by Rigilus if need be and if he were willing—and into them I would inculcate day and night by every possible human and mechanical means, the need for revenge! I would educate them upon nothing else but revenge and the scientific powers necessary to accomplish that revenge. That all of you can so lightly set aside the monstrous injustice that has been done to us is something that I cannot understand!"

"One as soulless as you never *will* understand," one of the women answered quietly.

"I am not soulless," Merva answered, coolly. "I am merely efficient. But I am the last one to attempt to judge my own character. I will leave it to you, Rigilus, to say what kind of a woman I am."

"Hard, my dear," Rigilus smiled. arising from his deep meditations. "Hard as a diamond, yet just as brilliant. Like you, though, I am somewhat puzzled by this humane streak which has developed in the rest of our friends. And not for one moment do I accede. I have stated what must be done and as the commander of the ship I order that there be no diversion from that instruction. You will see to it that progeny are produced and that the necessary doctrine is inoculated in them."

"No," Randos said, shaking his head. "We are firmly resolved on that, and any attempt on your part to force the issue, Rigilus, will make things decidedly unpleasant all round."

Merva Ansof sprang to her feet, a tall lioness of a woman, her fists clenched at her sides. Fiercely she looked round on her colleagues, her marble-white face set with the most ferocious determination.

"Do all of you dare suggest that we crawl out into the void like spineless amoeba, without intelligence, or without the capacity to inflict reprisal upon those who have condemned us to this fate?

"Can you, as men and women of the past regime, so completely forget that Rigilus gave us all the power of the solar system and yet now, when he asks you for the means to give strength back to the future generations, you refuse to comply? You should be ashamed of yourselves, every one of you!"

Rigilus had risen too, standing beside the incensed woman. His massive hand gently touched her arm.

"This is a matter which cannot be done by compulsion," he said, quietly, "only by co-operation. The fact remains that if no progeny are produced our plan of vengeance is useless anyway, because we shall all die in this space machine long before the journey is completed and with our dying, the tale will have been told.

"Consider it another way, my friends," he continued, looking on the serious faces around him. "Supposing you follow out the course which you wish—supposing children are born aboard this vessel. They are bound, in course of time, to ask many questions, many of them awkward ones, especially as to why they are living aboard a space ship when they ought to be living on the surface of a planet."

"They will never know that they should be living on the face of a planet unless we tell them so," Randos pointed out.

Rigilus shook his head. "You know better than that, my friend. Inherent in every human being is the instinct of where he ought to live, and if he is not in the conditions which are normal to his environment, he is bound sooner or later to wonder why, and inevitably he will ask those whom he feels do know the answer. You will be forced to the point finally of admitting that you have been banished from the world where you ought to be and I hardly think I need add what your children's reactions will be to that.

"They will have within them, knowing you as I do, the proud arrogance of those who have been masters, and they will not be inclined to lie down to the simple truth that their parents have been banished from a planet and nothing has been done about it. It is then that you will appreciate the wisdom of my doctrine. So I beg of you to forget this sentimentality—this archaic inclination to forgive your enemies—and bring into the world future men and women who can hand on to their children the knowledge of how to hit back. We have done nothing of which we need be ashamed. If that were so I would not be so insistent on this scheme of revenge. All that we did was build up the civilisations of Earth from the lowliest beginnings to the greatest of heights. For that we have been banished to the furthest deeps of the Universe and for that we rightly demand a price. Now my friends, make your choice!"

"It is not a case of making a choice, Rigilus," one of the men responded, pondering. "If we refuse to accede to your demand there is absolutely nothing you can do about it. Even if we have children after that, your doctrines need not necessarily be inculcated into them. We can stop that if we choose."

"How?" Merva Ansof snapped. "You seem to have overlooked the fact that Rigilus I is the commander of the vessel and still your Ruler. There is nothing that you dare do to him!"

"Why not?" Randos asked pointedly. "He is flesh and blood the same as us. There are ten of us against him so we can destroy him if we wish and if the circumstances were sufficiently serious we *would* do. What you do not seem to appreciate is, that now we have cut adrift from Earth and all its associations and so-called civilised fabric, we want to live like normal human beings without the need to dominate others, to have our own children, to live together and to teach those children whatever we feel they should know. We don't want to begin on the deadly basis that only vengeance is worth having."

Rigilus sighed heavily and turned aside. He moved slowly across to the great window and stood looking down on the receding Earth. Already it was no more than a globe as the enormous space liner fled with an apparent complete lack of movement through space. Then Merva Ansof moved also, an epitome of feline grace as she swept across the floor, pausing at length at the Ruler's side.

"You can't let them get away with this, Rigilus," she murmured, quietly, "you know you can't!"

"Ten of them against me," he said with a brief glance. "What am I supposed to do about that? A man can only enforce his will if he has a certain amount of co-operation and a certain amount of backing. I have only got you, apparently. Two of us against ten?" He shrugged his enormous shoulders. "We have to accept circumstances some-times, Merva."

"I never accept circumstances." Merva looked down on the Earth for a few moments, her green eyes seeming even greener with the emerald reflections cast back from the Mother planet. Rigilus glanced towards her. She was an extraordinarily beautiful woman—that fact he had always known—but the repellent coldness of her and the mer-ciless logic of her mind had always turned him against her from the emotional standpoint. Otherwise he and Merva Ansof would long ago have been joined in a union of world control.

"The solution," Merva said, presently, her voice deep and qui-et, "is far more simple than you think, Rigilus. Let these fools who were once all for us have their progeny. Even let these children be educated for several years as exactly as their parents wish. Let them think that they're getting away with it…. Whenever necessary there is nothing to stop the removal of the parents!"

Rigilus gave a start. "You cleverly avoid the use of the word 'murder', my dear," he commented.

"Murder is a silly, simple word, which dates back over a centu-ries. In these days murder is classed as elimination and that is not a matter of the passions: it is a matter of necessity. If anybody or anything stands in the way of achieving a certain objective, destroy it! That has always been my policy, Rigilus, and it has placed me beside you and there I have remained as long as I have been mature. Even as a child I eliminated the things that annoyed me. I sometimes think I am one of the few people who are gifted with a complete lack of conscience."

With that, using a typical feminine cunning, Merva Ansof turned and walked to another window to survey the unholy prominences of the blinding sun. She knew she had left behind a very undecided ex-ruler. She had dropped into his mind the seed that she knew must flourish. Rigilus loved power every bit as much as she did, and his desire for vengeance was something he was prepared to bring to fruition no matter what the cost. And presently he turned. Majestic as an eagle, his keen eyes peering out from under the overhanging brows.

"I am inclined to think," he said, slowly, "that perhaps you have a better grasp of the situation than I on this occasion, Randos."

Randos gave a start of hope and glanced quickly at the others. Immediately every face turned towards Rigilus as he came forward once again into the centre of the lounge.

"Yes," Rigilus continued, "have your children, by all means. I give you my word that I will make no attempt to indoctrinate them, but will give you absolute freedom to do as you wish with them, until they reach the age of maturity. When, however, they have reached the time when they are capable of assessing the situation for themselves I insist that it must be put to them whether or not reprisal should be sought upon those who have driven us into outer space.

"In that way they will not be influenced by me or by you, but will make their own decision. I do not for a single moment doubt what their decision will be, because as I said earlier they will have an inherited instinct concerning the situation and the sense of domination which they will inherit from you, will I think, make them determined to hand on to their own children the doctrine of which I have spoken.... But that is in the future. For the time being continue as you will. We cannot afford in this small circle here—for although you may not have realised it yet—each one of us is bound to be with the other until the day we die—any sign of friction whatever. The more we are compelled to be in each other's company the more necessary it is that we keep things on an even keel."

By the window as she looked out towards the Moon, Merva Ansof smiled to herself. Rigilus I had done exactly as she had anticipated he would.

CHAPTER TWO

PLAN FOR SURVIVAL

SO began the strange odyssey of the twelve from Earth. With resistless power the space machine soon passed from the orbit of Mars, and ere long even the red planet was forgotten as the orbits of Jupiter, Uranus, Saturn, Neptune and little Pluto were all passed in turn and the vessel travelled on into the true interstellar deeps and the inconceivably distant Alpha Centauri.

These relatively small distances across the Solar System were covered in a matter of a few months. Months in which the twelve spent their time orientating themselves to the new conditions. To a certain extent this was not a particularly difficult task since life was very little different from what it had been on Earth, the ship being a complete city within itself.

The only thing which was missing and which Merva Ansof felt, perhaps more than anybody, except perhaps Rigilus—was the need to control the progress and the behaviour of the masses. Here there was nothing to do but please themselves and do whatever they wished whenever they wished. Even at this point with only a few months gone by Rigilus was brought home to realising the sinister truth behind the People's Prosecutor's statement when he said that banishment was the worst punishment that could possibly befall a man of so dominant a personality as Rigilus.

He had become moody and restless, finding little to interest him since everything aboard the ship was more or less automatic and made no demands upon the scientific ingenuity for which he was remarkable. What particularly appalled him was the thought that the doctrine upon which heart was so set could not possibly start to even be mooted for many years yet.

Then as he was in one of these moods of black depression there drifted to his side the subtly smiling Merva Ansof. As usual she was gowned exquisitely in a sheath-like garment of vermillion red. Such was the warmth of the great lounge, her alabaster white shoulders and arms were bare and the sunlight cast through the window upon the absolute maturity of her bosom. She was a woman voluptuous to a degree, not only in the matter of sex, but in the matter of mind and the matter of power. For Merva Ansof the loss of the control of the Earthly solar system meant little: she had the sort of mind that could grasp even at universal power, and if possible gain it.

"Is something troubling you, Rigilus?" Her soft husky voice broke upon him as he gazed with troubled eyes through the great window upon the depths of space, now dusted with a host of shining stars.

He glanced towards her and, for a moment, even his almost impervious senses were shaken by the picture of carnal attractiveness that she presented.

"Naturally something is troubling me." His voice sounded unnaturally curt as he endeavoured to cover up his emotions. "It is this absolute lack of anything to do which is grinding me down. I have always been a man of energy, one who must always be doing something, one who must have whole worlds to juggle with and whole nations to control. That I should have to sit here like a God on the Heights of Olympus, staring down on to the immensities of space without the power to command that space is something so bitter that I am lost for words."

"In that," Merva said gently, "you reveal a complete lack of discipline over your mind, Rigilus. You do not find me bemoaning my fate. You do not find me looking out over space and saying that I can't control it. I never look on anything which I cannot control!"

Rigilus looked at her sharply. This was a new mood even for Merva Ansof. He thought he had seen her in every possible emotional form, yet here was yet another phase of her complex and utterly merciless character.

She seated herself as he looked at her and the glow of light from the stars and the now distant sun set the soft texture of her sheath-like gown shimmering with a ruby brilliance.

"Rigilus," she said, with an almost poisonous gentleness, "you and I in our control of the Solar System have never really had the time to get to know one another properly, have we?"

"I had hardly ever considered that necessary," Rigilus responded, thinking. "We acted as two units in a thoroughly efficient machine and the necessity to know more of each other personally hardly entered into it."

"Not then, perhaps," Merva admitted, with a shrug of her satin-smooth shoulders, "but it enters into it *now* don't you think? The rest of these fools aboard this ship—those whom we trusted so much and who are now revealed as only thinking of themselves—are all married and intending to bring into this vessel reproductions of themselves, with their own limited little viewpoint and their ridiculous little sentimentalities which would make absolute nonsense of your own magnificent scheme of revenge. It is up to us Rigilus, to change all that.

"If they can have their progeny and instil into them their limited notions and doctrines of conscience and right living, why shouldn't we have our children and inculcate into them the things that we both are strong for vengeance upon those who drove us hither. By that," Merva Ansof continued, her green eyes flashing a brief glance, "I do not mean that we should for one moment abandon the plan which I suggested to you earlier on, namely the elimination of the parents when the children have reached an age when they can be educated into understanding what we want them to understand. Meantime there is surely no reason why we cannot have children of our own, who can take over a leadership when we ourselves find we are getting beyond that."

"In other words," Rigilus said rather bluntly "what you're suggesting is marriage?"

"Naturally. I cannot imagine two people more suited to each other than you or I, Rigilus. You have the immense masculine strength and the power and I—," Merva looked down at herself and gave a faint, almost tigerish smile, "—and I am obviously a woman, with every wile and subtlety that the name implies."

As Rigilus didn't answer but still continued to look out of the window Merva rose to her feet and began to move slowly about the lounge. Rigilus did not watch her but he heard the soft silken rustle of her garments as she moved.

"I am not attempting to force anything upon you," she said after a while, "I am merely suggesting it as the most commonsense move in the situation in which we now find ourselves. You and I want revenge and we mean to have it. But if something unexpected came along and the pair of us were wiped out of existence it would be nice to know that we had others who would carry on the plan for us even if we could not.

"All this, of course, is assuming that anything might happen to us before the children of our colleagues reach an impressionable age. For the furtherance of your plan, Rigilus, we have *got* to have children of our own, and from the very moment that they become able to comprehend things the doctrine of vengeance must be instilled into them."

"You hardly sound like a potential mother-to-be," Rigilus commented at last. "In fact you sound to me more like a machine deciding how many cogs it needs to make itself efficient."

"Never mind what I sound like," Merva replied, coldly, "confine yourself instead to the commonsense of the suggestion I have made! In fact, consider yourself fortunate that a man of your domination and character should have a woman offering herself to him! Few women come towards you, Rigilus, because you frighten them. There's a tremendous strength and purpose about you that the normal woman finds almost repugnant I should imagine. I though, being of a totally different calibre, can appreciate it.

"What is more, I want to know more about it. What is even more important I desire that the union of the mind that we have had so long in the control of other people's destinies should now be a union that will reproduce a reproduction of ourselves. I shall not put forward the suggestion again. All that I await is your answer."

Rigilus was still silent. Not that there was really any point in him withholding his answer for he knew exactly what he was going to say. He had never in his life refused Merva Ansof, and he did not intend to refuse her now. He had never quite fathomed why he had always bowed to her suggestions because he was anything but a man of weak will or undeveloped individuality.

Deep down he wondered if it was because he was *afraid* of Merva Ansof. She was so unlike any other woman he had ever known. He turned at last and saw her standing looking at him, her green eyes with their long eyelashes wide and intent. Again the thought crossed his mind, was she a hypnotist? No, not that, he decided. Merva Ansof's secret lay in her tremendous subtlety and all the snake-like vice of which her sex was capable.

"Yes," Rigilus said, almost simply. "I do believe that union between us might be a very sensible idea."

She came forward at that and her dead white hands rested on his as they gripped the edge of the enormous window ledge.

"You will not have cause to regret this, Rigilus," she said, quietly. "Your aims and ambitions always have been and always will be mine too."

Rigilus nodded slowly.

"We shall tell the others, of course?"

"Of course. What else can we do? And as master of the ship you will have to perform the ceremony. I should imagine the others will be glad of our union. It will make us so much like—what is the old world phrase? One big happy family...."

Typically Rigilus wasted no more time. Leaving the lounge he headed through the main corridor to the big solarium where the rest of the party was gathered and coming into their midst, made his announcement. He had just come to the end of it when Merva Ansof herself came silently through the doorway and stood looking upon the others with that curiously mocking smile which she could use so effectively.

"Naturally," Randos said, rising to his feet, "we are both delighted and encouraged, Rigilus, that you should have decided upon this course. The only thing that has surprised me is that you and Merva did not marry long ago."

"So long as we do it now," Merva herself remarked, "what does that matter? The need of marriage was not so great when we were on the Earth as it is now that we are outcasts in space. There remains nothing now, Rigilus," she added, glancing towards him, "but for you to perform the ceremony. The old necessity of witnesses and so forth is eliminated by the fact that those of us here comprise the only world we know, or are ever likely to know again."

Rigilus nodded slowly, seeming as though he found it difficult to absorb the fact that this giant space liner cleaving the silent depths was indeed their only world for all time to come. Then gathering himself together he went across to the nearby bookshelf, took down the Bible—still accepted among Earth People as a criterion for absolute solemnization—and came back again to where Merva was standing. In a matter of a moment he had recited the few lines necessary to make his marriage to Merva Ansof entirely legal, then from the little finger of his left hand he withdrew a small circlet of gold and slipped it upon Merva's third finger as she held out her hand towards him.

"All legal and complete," he remarked, smiling at her seriously. "I am afraid, my dear, that if you are expecting anything in the nature of a romance you are going to be sadly disappointed. I am not a romantic man and never have been."

"I don't want a romantic man," Merva answered, studying the ring. "All I require is a man who has power, which, as his wife I can share."

Such was the simple nature of the initial ceremony, so simple indeed that the remaining members of the banished party very soon forgot all about it. They accepted the day by day routine as a natural part of their lives and it was perfectly obvious from the remarks they passed now and again that they had entirely lost all remembrance of Rigilus' original statement concerning the scheme of vengeance.

For that matter Merva herself did not mention it either. She was quite content to bide her time, knowing that she was now in a quite unassailable position as the wife of Rigilus, and naturally she was quite determined that she would press her own case to the uttermost when, with the passage of years, the time arose to make the elimination of the unwanted ones necessary.

Not that she was idle as the days and months fled by and not only Earth but the entire Solar System retired into the infinite depths of space and was lost to sight amidst the constellations which formed the backdrop behind it.

"I am surprised, Rigilus," she commented one morning as she came upon him at work in the enormous laboratory in the centre of the vessel, "that you accept so completely the fact that we can never complete our journey to Alpha Centauri."

He glanced at her, giving his serious smile.

"I cannot see that there is anything in that to occasion surprise, Merva. As you are aware, we are no longer accelerating, but moving at a constant velocity. Since our speed is far below the speed of light, it is an irrefutable fact that neither you nor I—nor any of us aboard this ship for that matter—can live for the thousand years it will take to reach Alpha Centauri."

"Are you absolutely sure of that?"

Rigilus hesitated, vaguely puzzled. He had always known Merva as a woman of extremely brilliant scientific ideas, and therefore one absolutely steeped in logic. That she should even assume to question the fact that he or herself could live for a thousand years was extraordinary.

"Of course I'm sure of it," he answered at length, "and so must you be."

"Matter of fact I'm not." Merva reclined against the edge of the enormous machine bench. "I've been giving a great deal of thought to the matter during the last few weeks Rigilus. I have been thinking how wonderful it would be if you and I were still alive and in perfect condition mentally and physically at the end of our colossal journey. By that time we would have developed the mightiest scheme of vengeance that ever was.

"We might even have worked out the necessary mathematics to take us back across space at almost the speed of light, infinitely faster than our outward journey. The fuel is there, that we know, therefore the only thing that is needed is the necessary scientific ingenuity to defeat the blight of old age."

"You don't ask much," Rigilus commented drily. "You should know that for many years now we have been at work trying to find out how to create synthetic life, but all our endeavours came to nothing. I think you are wasting your time in hoping for a life of a thousand years."

"I never waste my time in talking about anything which is not capable of realisation," Merva replied deliberately, "hear me out while I tell you my plan.

"There exists in every normal human being up to the age of about ten a tremendous life energy. You should be aware of that from the findings of scientists of as far back as nearly a hundred years ago. It was a Russian scientist whose name I forget who first made the discovery whilst engaged upon a complicated operation which demanded the transplanting of a young heart into an old body."

"Yes, I am quite informed upon such experiments," Rigilus assented, his brow clouding somewhat.

"Very well then. Why should that experiment be lost in the medical annals of the past when we can turn it to such advantage? There never was a more desperate need for all the medical and scientific skill we can bring into use. As I understood it the transplanting of the young heart into the old body was just a straightforward operation. What really emerged from that experiment was the fact that this Russian scientist was able to positively prove that from a young body there emanates a form of energy totally different from that of a body that is adolescent or mature.

"Anyway, he found there was enough of the energy to cause a reaction upon the electrical instruments he was using. The later treatise he wrote showed that the energy was not confined to that one particular body but exists in all young ones up to approximately the age of ten years from the moment of birth."

"Well," Rigilus enquired, still puzzled. "How does that affect us in our particular case?"

"It helps us in this way. Since that energy is available it must surely be capable of transmission from one body to the other—in other words a kind of energy blood transfusion, if you know what I mean. If blood can be transferred from one person to another by mechanical means, then I'm perfectly sure that energy can be transferred from one person to another by *electrical* means.

"What I am suggesting is this: when the children of our colleagues have reached the age of about five years they should be capable of giving forth all the young and vital energy which we require. Between now and that time we have plenty of opportunity to build the necessary electrical equipment which should be able to absorb and store that bodily energy which can afterwards be transferred to us. By that I mean you and me. That should have the effect of counterbalancing the incessant breakdown of cells and loss of energy which is the ultimate cause of old age and death."

"Your plan," Rigilus said, after a moment or two's reflection, "has all the brilliance which I have come to expect from you. Have you, however, thought what will happen if we withdraw from them vital energy? It is more than possible that they will die because of it. Nature put that energy there for a reason and its removal might bring about their death."

"Would that matter?" Merva asked, shrugging.

"I think it would," Rigilus retorted. "I don't wish to see the death of our children. I understood that they were to be brought into being for the sole purpose of carrying on the plan of vengeance upon which we are both agreed."

"I am not talking about *our* children," Merva retorted; "I said the children of our colleagues, which is a very different thing. They don't concern us; they are merely the offspring of those who have proved disloyal to us when it comes to the execution of a scheme of revenge. My original idea was to inculcate into them the plan of vengeance against Earth, but how much better it will be if we ourselves can carry out that plan a thousand years hence.

"Use the children for energy purposes only, destroy the parents who will be bound to raise objections and finally it will leave only you and me, Rigilus, given almost eternal life—and most certainly life which will last for a thousand years—and if there are others besides us they will be our own children who will be wholly in agreement with our plans. If they are *not* in agreement then they must be eliminated."

"Evidently," Rigilus remarked with a wistful smile, "I was right when I said you regarded children as nothing more than cogs in a machine and if the whole machine does not function perfectly because some of those cogs are not suitable, they must be destroyed. That is what it amounts to, isn't it?"

"Entirely," Merva assented. "At least, the scheme is a good one; you must admit that."

"Yes, I admit it," Rigilus conceded, sighing. "The only thing I am wondering about is if the chance to live a thousand years would be appreciated. For myself even though only a matter of months have gone by since we left the Earth I am already completely wearied with the monotony of this space journeying. The very thought of a thousand years of it makes me feel inclined to open the airlock at this very moment and fling myself into the void."

"That," Merva said, with a contemptuous smile, "is nothing else but defeatism, and I am surprised that a man of your rugged strength should even contemplate it Rigilus. Let us have no more of it: let us concentrate instead upon the scientific possibilities of the idea that I have put forward. Let us use all the resources of this great laboratory here for the creation of the necessary electrical equipment to absorb life energy. There will come a time when the first children will begin to appear amongst us and from that moment onwards our plan will start to move slowly but inevitably towards its climax."

Rigilus nodded assent because there as nothing else he could do, though inwardly he did not agree with Merva's almost horrifying conception of absorption of life energy; he was on the other hand the creator of the original scheme of vengeance and therefore he certainly could not back out at this juncture. Later there might come a chance to turn Merva from her chosen course but right at this moment there was nothing else Rigilus could do but fall in with her wishes.

"Have you any preconceived ideas on what kind of equipment we ought to construct?" he enquired.

"Certainly I have; in fact, more than that, I have blueprints. Here, see them for yourself...."

Rigilus stood watching in some surprise as from the pocket of her silken one-piece garment Merva took a folded sheet of graph paper and spread it out on the bench.

Rigilus studied it, noting immediately the immense attention to scientific details that had always been Merva's strong point.

"Since at the moment there are no children aboard," she said after a moment or two, "we have no means of determining the amount of energy they give off. You will see from this apparatus here that I have allowed for that and have constructed it very much on the principle of one of the ordinary power-absorbers used in our laboratories back on Earth. The energy is picked up by this magnetic brush system and is then stored up as potential for release when required. I'm absolutely convinced that such an appartus ought to work admirably."

Of this, as far as Rigilus could see, there was very little doubt, so without any more hesitation he began to gather together all the materials for the actual construction of the machine that Merva had designed.

During this time they saw but little of their old colleagues, except at the generally accepted meal times. A system of shifts and reliefs had of course been arranged so that somebody or other was always moving about the ship constantly on guard in case of the arrival of some sudden meteorite which might cause irreparable disaster to the ship, or on the other hand there might be some form of cosmic life which would make itself apparent and would need destroying. For, although the party aboard the ship—with the exception of Rigilus and Merva—knew that they would never see a planet again, they still did not wish to die prematurely through the advent of the unexpected. Hence the constant guard against the possibility of sudden disaster.... But nothing ever happened.

In this time the Earthly Solar System had become so remote that it had disappeared altogether and the Sun was little better than a pinpoint star in far off infinity. Ahead, the enormous galaxies of the Universe never seemed to come any nearer so stupendous was their distance away. The ship flew on and on, consuming hardly any power since it was still maintaining the same velocity it had achieved when the engine was cut off.

And so the circumscribed little world flew onwards, carrying with it ten souls who were entirely, or almost entirely, content with their lot and looking forward to the arrival of their children ere very long, and two others who were plotting and planning to defeat the ravages of time that they might live a thousand years. In the passage of months Rigilus had had to a great extent come round to Merva's way of thinking in regard to this and the interest of building and testing the equipment for life energy had to a great extent alleviated the crushing sense of monotony which had been ruling him. For this reason, if for none other, he was very much the man of action he had been when ruler of the Earth and the Solar System.

But if either Rigilus or Merva imagined that their scientific or constructional work had entirely escaped the notice of their colleagues they were quite mistaken. The ever-watchful Randos, who was more or less considered to be the self-appointed leader of those outside Rigilus and Merva, had more often than not asked himself what the strange device was in the laboratory upon which Rigilus and Merva spent so much time.

Neither of them were aware that whilst they had been absent during their sleeping periods Randos had made it his business to very carefully examine the apparatus until he had arrived at a very definite conclusion as to its purpose. He could not be absolutely certain that it was intended for the storage of life-energy, but being a scientist of fair ability he could at least form a theory. Nor did he consider that it was out of place for him to question Rigilus and Merva outright.

He did so in the most casual manner, arriving in the laboratory one morning—'morning' being entirely governed by the chronometer, since in space there was nothing but eternal night and starshine. Both Rigilus and | Merva were at work upon the apparatus in question when Randos presented himself, and they could tell immediately from the grimness of his expression something of extreme moment was on his mind.

"I assume," he asked, as Rigilus and Merva looked at him in surprise, "that no regulation has been made to prevent me or anybody eke entering this laboratory?"

"No regulation at all," Rigilus assented; "you are quite welcome my friend. Naturally you must have something with which to pass the time."

"It's not a matter of that," Randos looked about him quickly. "I have my own particular hobbies with which I am able to while away the endless hours…. It just so happens that I am particularly interested in that apparatus upon which you and your wife are engaged."

"What concern is it of yours?" Merva asked him shortly, staring at him with her wide green eyes.

"It is my concern because I cannot possibly see any reason for building an electrical apparatus when we have around us every kind of equipment we can possibly need."

"In other words," Merva asked, "just plain curiosity, is that it?"

"Frankly, yes." Randos looked at her squarely. "I am not an absolute novice in understanding scientific equipment and it is perfectly obvious that equipment is intended for the absorption of energy. At first I thought that perhaps you were intending to absorb cosmic energy, the only type of energy in existence in this far flung quarter of space. Certainly it could not be solar energy that you are intending to tamper with. Then when I came to study the apparatus more closely I could see that it was not built for absorbing the immense voltage which cosmic energy would take; that suggests to me that there is only one other form of energy that it could be intended to deal with— Life energy."

Rigilus came forward slowly. "From the sound of things, my friend, you have spent quite a lot of time in this laboratory when my wife and I have not been present."

"Is there any particular law against that?"

"No; but I would appreciate it if you would confine yourself to your own particular hobbies and leave the activities of my wife and myself alone."

"That I am quite prepared to do, but I cannot help but feel from the urgent resentment which has suddenly come into your manner that you are both engaged upon some kind of apparatus which does not bode very well for the rest of us."

"Stop being so ridiculous," Merva answered, coldly.

"Is there any reason," Randos asked, ignoring her and looking straight at Rigilus, "why this apparatus you are working on cannot be explained to the rest of us? Why has it been kept a secret for so long? It is obviously an equipment of very extreme intricacy, and since it is intended for life energy, there can only be one set of human beings for whom it is intended—children. Life energy, according to the researches of past scientists, and indeed our own laboratory technicians, does not exist in any individual after the age of ten years. Could it be," Randos asked deliberately, his mouth hardening, "that you are aiming at some particularly ingenious scientific trick which will only reveal itself when our children are born?"

"I do not propose to answer any questions," Rigilus said, curtly, "and I would be glad if you will leave us immediately!"

Randos smiled rather tautly, inclined his head and departed. The moment he had gone Merva turned quickly, her eyes glittering as she looked at Rigilus.

"That man is dangerous, Rigilus. He knows far too much. You must take the necessary steps to have him silenced. We underestimated his capabilities as a scientific analyst, and evidently he knows as much about life energies as we do. He is liable to spread any sort of story amongst the others and once that happens we can expect trouble, and the only way we can defeat trouble is to smash it halfway."

"By doing what?" Rigilus asked, moodily. "You don't suppose that I can suddenly go into their midst, single Randos out and kill him, do you?"

"No, I don't see any necessity for anything quite so blatant as that," Merva agreed, "but there is certainly nothing to prevent his meeting with an accident, and quickly, too, before he can talk too much. He always has been a man with an enquiring turn of mind and if he has too much to say it will mean ten against us and that will take a good deal of handling. You'll have to act at once!"

Rigilus hesitated, plainly uncertain. Merva looked at him steadily, waiting, then as he made no move she made a quick gesture of annoyance.

"This isn't a matter that can wait, Rigilus! Since you won't act—I shall—and now!"

She wasted no further time. Hurrying from the laboratory she overtook Randos who was moving at a languid pace along the immense corridor that ran through the heart of the vessel. He turned as Merva came hurrying up and looked at her in sardonic inquiry.

"Is there something I can do for the wife of the Ruler?" he asked, cynically.

Immediately Merva's mood changed from that to which everyone was accustomed. Instead she switched on extreme plaintiveness that even the wily Randos could not entirely resist.

"I feel that I owe you an apology, Randos," Merva said. "I was downright rude to you back in the laboratory there, considering you were only asking a perfectly normal question. My husband and I have been working so hard on that apparatus that it has made us rather less courteous than usual. I do hope that you will forgive me."

Randos merely shrugged and waited for the next.

"Since you asked so many questions," Merva continued, "you are entitled to the answers and I feel that I am the best one to give them to you since the idea of building a machine to capture life energy is mine. Would you care to step into the sub-laboratory for a moment where I can explain more fully?"

Randos nodded, not for a moment expecting anything.

Upon which Merva turned to the nearby doorway that led on to a contiguous region of the main laboratory and stepped into the great instrument-lined space beyond,

Randos following behind her and looked about him with interest. He had already been in here before and knew pretty well all the apparatus contained therein. How any of it could apply to the life energy equipment that was in the main laboratory he had yet to discover.

"The one thing which you must understand," Merva said, seriously, "is that the life energy equipment which we are now building has nothing whatever to do with the children which you and the other men and their wives are expecting to bring amongst us shortly. It is concerned entirely with the progeny of Rigilus and myself. Our idea is to capture some of this life energy and by its means we can perhaps extend the so-called normal span of our lives to double or treble the accepted amount."

"At least I thank you for telling me," Randos said, gravely. "I do feel though that you are making an extreme mistake in attempting to tamper with an energy which Nature alone gives."

"It is quite possible that we are wrong in our calculations," Merva admitted, "but we cannot possibly determine that until we have experimented. Certainly we will see that nobody comes to any harm because of our endeavours.

"In here," she continued, moving to one of the machines, "is a subsidiary equipment which we have perfected and which no doubt in your travels around you have already seen!"

Randos shook his head as he looked around him. "Even if I have seen it I have not recognized it. Which one is it?"

Merva pointed to a squat, many-dialled apparatus upon the top of which were electro-magnetic devices.

"This is it," she said, simply, switching a button so that the apparatus hummed steadily, "and with it in action you can see for yourself exactly how we propose to absorb the energy. That is, of course, the whole business on a very small scale, but at least it will give you the idea."

Randos nodded interestedly and stepped forward. Merva seemed to consider something carefully and then nodded towards a massive switch on the apparatus.

"Actually this is a job for two to handle," she explained. "You pull that switch down and I'll move this lever here and then we have the first stage of the theoretical experiment complete."

Randos did exactly as he was ordered and pulled the switch. Immediately Merva moved the lever she had referred to from left to right with savage vigour. The result was that Randos gave a tremendous gasp of anguish as a colossal electrical current surged through him, flashing from the soles of his boots, along the metal floor on which he was standing. Even Merva herself caught some of the electrical impact and was flung backwards to land heavily on her face some feet away. When at length she felt sufficiently recovered, she sat up and looked about her to behold Randos sprawled helplessly on the floor in front of the softly humming machine.

"Unfortunate," she commented to herself, rising, "but very necessary."

With that she left the machine running, walked in a wide circle round the fallen Randos and so out into the corridor again and back to the laboratory. Rigilus looked at her enquiringly as she entered and he could not help the feeling of emotional disturbance that passed through him as he studied the unholy smile on her face.

"I think," she said, catching his glance, "that Randos will not disturb us again, and to the best of my knowledge there is nobody else scientific enough amongst our colleagues to even have the vaguest idea what we are driving at."

"What have you *done* to Randos?" Rigilus demanded, catching Merva's shoulders and shaking her fiercely.

"Eliminated him," she answered coldly, snatching herself free, "and I'll thank you to keep your hands off me Rigilus!"

Rigilus dropped his hands and looked at her steadily from beneath his tufted eyebrows.

"Just what did you do? I may as well know."

"I had the fool pull down the main switch on one of the electrical storage generators. I rather feared he would suspect the trick but he didn't. He did exactly as I told him and the second the main switch was on and the potential lever released he naturally got the full voltage and that was that! It will look as though he went into the laboratory and set the thing going for himself, not taking the necessary precautions to save himself from electrocution."

Rigilus tightened his lips.

"You certainly mean to enforce your will by whatever means you can, don't you, Merva?"

She nodded calmly. "Certainly I do. And there will probably have to be quite a few accidents before we have the children of these fools entirely in our hands. I am quite prepared for that and if you do not like what I am doing, Rigilus, it is possible that even you might run into trouble."

Rigilus stared at her for a moment and then laughed shortly.

"You against me? Don't be absurd my dear. I would very soon discover any machinations which you might plan against me."

"So you imagine," she retorted. "There is one thing which you must understand, Rigilus, and that is, that I am determined this plan of vengeance shall be executed no matter who tries to prevent it. I've had the feeling all along that you are no longer so keen on the plan as you were and for that reason I must see to it that you do not lose your enthusiasm. If you do and it is left entirely to me to carry the plan through then at least you can die feeling that your mission has been left in good hands."

CHAPTER THREE

MERVA STRIKES

THE death of Randos was accepted without question as an accident for the simple reason that it never occurred to the more simple minded members forming the rest of the banished ones that neither Rigilus or Merva would descend to the level of murder, for murder was one of the most outmoded of crimes long since destroyed in the civilisation of Earth by the concentrated work of medical specialists and psychiatric experts.

The only one who did have the vaguest suspicion and yet could not do anything about it was Randos' wife, but even she was disarmed by the immense superficial sympathy which Merva poured upon her and at last even she came to think that the whole business must have been an accident so splendidly did Merva play her delusive part.

Certainly nobody else asked any questions about the life energy equipment, even though none of them was prevented from studying it during the times when Merva and Rigilus were off duty and thereby unable to guard the laboratory....

And the weeks and the months passed by. With the life energy machine now completed there were no further experiments for Merva and Rigilus to engage upon. There was nothing they could do but wait until the slow maturity of the few children that had been born in the past few days had reached a reasonable maximum thereby enabling them to become suitable subjects for the transmission of life current.

There also came a further hiatus in the life of Merva herself when her own child was born. It proved to be a son, with the green eyes and black hair of his mother. Rigilus was not sure whether he was pleased by the event or not. He felt somehow that if necessary his ruthless wife would not hesitate to sacrifice her own child to the ideal of revenge if necessity compelled it. But this was something far too early to decide as yet, so he behaved just as any father might when at length Merva was up and about again and the recipient of congratulations from the remainder of the banished people.

Merva herself seemed somewhat changed after the birth of her son in that her manner was less harsh and indeed even sympathetic at times. What Rigilus did not grasp in his masculine bluntness was that Merva was merely lulling everybody else in the ship into a sense of false security—giving them a totally wrong impression of her character—so that the life energy experiment when it was finally conducted would seem not to attach so much to her, as a mother herself, as to Rigilus. Merva well knew that Rigilus had been the first to expound the plan of vengeance and had made each of his colleagues register that vow before departing from Earth, that they would implement the plan of revenge that he had outlined. It would therefore not seem unusual when the children of the colleagues were subjected to the life energy experiment that he was the prime mover in the whole scheme.

If there was any trouble—as Merva fully anticipated there would be—it would be Rigilus who would catch the full blast of it. Not that this concerned her in the least now. By him she had had her son, which was all that mattered, and this son could very easily take the place of Rigilus as the years passed and there was granted to her the eternality of life produced by the life energy of other children in whom she had not the remotest interest.

Rigilus, suspecting none of these things, went steadily on. He maintained a just control of the peoples in the space machine and they in turn behaved quite normally and caused no trouble whatever. Indeed, they had no need to as yet, for they were allowed to educate their children as they wished—and there were six children in all, three boys and three girls—which had brought into their lives an interest and lifted from them the crushing load of monotony produced by the everlasting journeying through space.

Inevitably there were times, as the months spread into years and Merva still waited her chance, when the children were old enough to ask questions concerning their strange environment. This was the very thing that Randos had predicted, but Rigilus was well ready for it. Still keeping to the promise he had made and securing beforehand

Merva's assent, he told the children the story of a vast exploration into the far deeps of space from the Mother World and said nothing whatever about the banishment which was the cause of it, or the plan of vengeance which must one day be brought to maturity....

And still the years passed on and the children grew. They were all brightly intelligent offspring, carefully educated in the arts of science by their doting parents and indeed having lavished upon them a great deal more attention than any normal children because there was nothing much else for their parents to do.

Rigilus and Merva's own child grew up alongside them, showing signs early of becoming tall and massive like his father, with a great deal of his majestic bearing, but having also the coldly individual indifference which was his mother's outstanding characteristic. Rigilus had little chance to converse or direct the mind of his own son: Merva always took the issues straight out of his hands, spending many hours inculcating into that pliable young mind the urgency and the need for revenge upon the successors of those who had brought about this banishment into the deeps of space.

As yet the boy, who had been given the unusual name of Exodus, was hardly able to take in the invective and venom which his mother poured into his mind, but she knew quite well what she was doing and she knew too, that as the mind gradually developed it would absorb and mature itself upon the facts which she had given. She hoped that when Exodus reached manhood he would be the living symbol of vengeance and would bring to bear all the scientific knowledge that had been given him upon the problem of revenge....

And still the years passed and the machine flew onwards with the same resistless, unchanging velocity.

Then at last came the day when Merva acted. She had by this time so satisfied the other members of the spaceship's community that she was entirely sympathetic towards their children that she had no difficulty in gathering them all about her with the apparent intention of taking them into the solarium to unfold to them one of those wildly imaginative stories for which she was remarkable.

Rigilus knew exactly what she intended doing but had no power whatever to stop her—or if he had he did not choose to use it. He had by this time come to realise only too clearly that his wife was entirely the dominant factor in their union. All he could do was to go to the laboratory at her summons and there he found her with the three boys and the three girls grouped around her and the throbbing energy of the life-energy machine already in operation.

"You intend then to carry it through?" he asked her briefly.

"Certainly I do, and shut and lock the door," she commanded.

He obeyed and came over to her, surveying the six innocent-eyed children with a certain air of resignation.

"Somehow," he said, heavily, "it seems a difficult thing now to use the young and hopeful lives in the furtherance of a scheme of vengeance. We are mature and full of hates and bitterness: these children are young and have the virtue of absolute innocence. Can you find it in your heart Merva, to still carry out the plan which you devised so many years ago?"

"Can I find it in my heart?" she repeated, gazing at him blankly with her green eyes. "What do you think I've been doing these past five years? I have been waiting, waiting, waiting! Longing for the day when I could ay last use the energy of these children to restore to me the energy and mental power, which is already beginning to show signs of waning.

"Do you know, Rigilus, I looked at myself in the mirror this morning and, just for a moment I could see the lines of time beginning to appear clearly upon my face and that was what prompted me to get the experiment under way before the chisel has the chance to dig any deeper. I cannot understand why you should even question the moves we are about to make. You seem to have forgotten that the idea was originally yours—"

"The idea of vengeance, yes," Rigilus interrupted. "But this ghastly scheme of trying to absorb the life energy of children was yours. I did not agree with it then and I do not agree with it now and if I could think of any way of stopping you short of murder. I would. In the years that have passed I have come to realise that nursing a grievance is nothing but slow destruction of the mind. It becomes even more pointless when one is most unlikely to see the result of one's planning."

Merva sighed. "From that I gather that you still do not realise that if we can get enough life-energy from these children you and I can go on through the years and see the plan come to a successful conclusion."

Rigilus sighed. "Space travelling so consistently has changed all that for me. The plan of revenge no longer interests me."

"In which case it is left for me to deal with," Merva said harshly, "and deal with it I shall!"

Turning aside she quickly ushered the wondering children forward until they were within range of the life-energy apparatus. Rigilus stood watching them in sad silence, trying meanwhile to make up his mind what he ought to do.

Merva ignored his deep meditation, switched on the apparatus, and then busied herself with the various control knobs. From long experience and numerous tests, which of course had not been made on any living beings, she knew the exact area of the machine's influence, which meant that the six children now standing before it would come directly within its baleful radius.

There was no time for Rigilus to decide what he must do for within a matter of moments the children had been absorbed in the instrument's strange power. The effect was exactly as Rigilus had once foreseen and which he felt sure Merva herself must have known would happen. The children simply dropped as though struck down with an invisible ray. They themselves had the experience of finding every vestige of their strength drained from them, the result of which was to stop the action of their hearts completely.

Not that this interested Merva: her eyes were fixed on the input dials of the instrument and at length she turned sharply towards where Rigilus was gazing in aghast silence at the six small bodies sprawled upon the metal floor.

"Look, Rigilus. A hundred per cent intake of energy," Merva exclaimed gripping his arm. "Every detail that we worked out has proved itself to be correct. There is enough energy stored here if used gradually over the years to give us life as prolonged as we can possibly wish." Merva looked at Rigilus intently as he hardly seemed to note what she was saying. Then suddenly her voice rose almost to an hysterical shout. "Don't you realise what I am *saying*, Rigilus? We have enough power here to—"

"Yes, yes, I heard you," Rigilus said, irritably, looking up at her. "And what of these children who have been destroyed in order that this destruction of old age might be accomplished? How are you going to explain that to their parents?"

She smiled bitterly. "You are going to explain that, Rigilus. I have every bit of it worked out, and in case you wonder what I mean it as simple as this...."

Before Rigilus could grasp what she had meant she suddenly swung to the instrument next to the life-energy machine and snapped on the control button. Rigilus had split seconds to understand what the second machine was. He had seen Merva constructing it at intervals through the years but had assumed, quite naturally, that it was intended as a protective mechanism, if the other members of the ship's colony showed signs of becoming dangerous. Certainly he had never suspected that it would be used against himself.

It was fashioned after the shape of a projector and emanated atomic vibration to the extent that it was capable of destroying the molecular structure of the flesh and bone. It could also destroy inorganic matter completely as Rigilus had already seen during past experiments. These were the only things he had time to remember then, her cruel face the picture of venom, Merva swung the lensed front of the instrument straight at him and pressed the button. Rigilus never knew what hit him. He was conscious of a brief and thundering pain that cascaded into total whirling darkness and his immense body crashed heavily to the floor.

Merva looked down at him but she did not switch the machine off; instead she raced to the door of the laboratory, yanked it open and called hoarsely down the long corridor.

"Come quickly, all of you! Quickly! Something terrible has happened!"

It was only a matter of moments before the men and women of the community came hurrying down the narrow vista in response to her cry, to finally come upon her in the laboratory to find her staring in horror at the fallen figure of Rigilus and the six children lying around him.

"What happened, Merva?" one of the men demanded, gripping her arm and shaking her.

Merva was the complete actress when she wanted. She merely looked at the man dazedly as though she were too horror-stricken to find words to express herself. Then she pointed to the fallen figures upon the floor. By this time the parents of the children were gathering up their respective offspring in their arms and there arose in the still quiet of the enormous space the grief-stricken cries of the women-folk and the bitter murmurings of the men.

"What happened?" demanded the man again, who was holding Merva.

At this she pulled herself free from his grip and moved to the atomic machine and switched it off. Then she turned and faced the men and women, looking at them fixedly.

"It was Rigilus," she said, in her low voice. "He must have been planning this moment for a long time. I brought the children in here intending to tell them a story as I have done for so many years when Rigilus suddenly came in and said he had an electrical experiment which he thought would entertain them. Before I could grasp what had happened he had projected this instrument at the children and it instantly killed them. I think that it was an accident for realising what he had done, he raced forward to examine them and himself came within range of the instrument and was stricken down even as they had been. Then I called for you...."

The men and women said nothing. With their various children in their arms they stood looking at Merva and she gazed back at them. She was still maintaining her act, her heavy bosom rising and falling emotionally as though she were struggling to get a grip of herself.

"I notice," one of the men remarked, glancing about him, "that your son Exodus is not here, Merva. Why was he not to be included in the telling of the story? As far as I can remember he has always been present when the other children have been. What was the merciful providence that saved him on this particular occasion?"

"He is busy studying," Merva replied. "It was just chance that he happened to be away, and needless to say I thank the Cosmos that he was. You must realise that the whole thing was an accident," she insisted. "What possible reason could Rigilus have had for wanting to kill these children of yours? Even more important, what possible reason could he have had for wanting to kill himself? The very nature of the tragedy shows that it was nothing else but mischance."

"I would like to believe that," one of the women said, holding her dead child close to her, "but for some reason I cannot. I have never felt particularly sanguine about you Merva. I have always felt that it was not Rigilus who ruled you but *you* who ruled *Rigilus*, and most certainly I cannot overlook the most extraordinary coincidence that saved your son Exodus from destruction when our children have perished."

The artificial look of terror suddenly vanished from Merva's face and she stood erect, coldly challenging.

"Do you dare to accuse me of having *arranged* this?" she demanded. "Have you the effrontery to accuse me?"

"I am not accusing anybody." the woman retorted, "I am merely remarking the coincidence. At the moment there is nothing that we can do but accept your word for it but I am sure you will not mind if we question Exodus as to why he was not among these children of ours when the disaster happened?"

"I'll permit you to do no such thing," Merva snapped. "I have given you my word and it is for you to accept it. I do not intend to stand here and be accused as the perpetrator of the tragedy that was brought about entirely by an unhappy accident. Naturally my condolences are with you—and don't forget that there is a considerable amount of bereavement attached to me also. Observe my husband lying there as dead as your children."

One of the other women, the limp form of her child in her arms, smiled bitterly. "I do not observe Merva, that your bereavement has touched you very deeply," she commented. "At first I was inclined to believe that your grief was genuine: now I have my doubts."

Merva waited for the next, her face set in hard lines, but none of the men and women in the assembly said anything further. Instead they looked at each other and then with a silent exchange of nods they went silently from the laboratory bearing their young dead with them.

Merva watched the door close silently behind them and afterwards stood for several moments in deep thought. Finally she looked down at the sprawled body of Rigilus and then she came to her decision. Certainly there was no room for a corpse aboard the space liner so inevitably the body of Rigilus would have to be treated to the same fate as had the body of Randos—but on this occasion Merva would have to do the task herself. Accordingly she crossed quickly to the laboratory door, opened it, then returned to where Rigilus was lying and began to drag him across the floor, a task which required considerable effort, for he was a big, heavy man. Knowing she could not call on any help from the others she continued with her task by easy stages until at last she had brought Rigilus' corpse to the every edge of the emergency trap which lay in the floor of the central corridor.

After that the rest was comparatively simple. Pressure on a button shot the trap in the floor to one side and a little manoeuvring dropped Rigilus' body into the cavity beneath. The moving of a second button closed the upper trap and opened the lower one, dropping the corpse into the frigid deeps of interstellar space.

Inevitably the corpse would constantly trail in the wake of the ship, chained by its mass gravity, nor was there any guarantee as to which exact position it would take up. Merva did not know, or care, whether the corpse would follow in the rear of the vessel, a constant accusing ghost, or whether it would follow beneath the machine and thereby be out of sight unless specially looked for. Whatever the possibilities, Rigilus was out of the way and she had gained all the potential energy she needed to produce an approach to near eternal life. Certainly enough energy to last a thousand years.

Smiling tautly to herself she continued along the corridor until she reached the chamber where she had left Exodus. She half expected to find him being questioned by other members of the party but this did not prove to be the case. He was seated on the ledge beneath the big porthole gazing out with a child's wonder on to the everlasting deeps.

In a moment or two his mother had crossed the room and seated herself at his side. She caught his hands possessively.

"Now you listen to me, Exodus," she said deliberately fixing her eyes upon him, "no matter what anybody else in the ship may say to you, no matter what questions they may ask you, you are to say that I told you to remain in here and study your books—until I returned to you. You understand me?"

"Yes, mother," Exodus answered simply. A child already well ahead of normal development, thanks to the high-pressure education which had been given to him almost since the first moment he had been able to comprehend his surroundings.

"If you do not do exactly as I have told you, you will make me very angry," Merva added, "and you know already, Exodus, what I am like when my anger is aroused."

"Yes mother," the child answered, again in the same voice, then turned his somewhat sad green eyes back to the void and contemplated the stars.

Merva looked at him searchingly for a moment, and then finally, satisfied that he would do exactly as she had ordered, she turned and left him, going back to the laboratory. Once here she made a careful examination of the life-energy apparatus and her original high hopes were more than confirmed as she came to study the input meters. There was no doubt that the absorption of energy from the six young children had produced a one hundred per cent current upon which she could draw as and when she wished, thereby giving unto herself a tide of almost ever-lasting life.

"And," she mused, surveying the instrument, "there is no better time to start than now. Fortunately for me none of these other fools are clever enough to understand the meaning of this apparatus, otherwise they would begin to realise as the years pass and I grow no older, the real purpose of this machine and the cause of the death of their children."

Wasting no more time she connected the wrist electrodes to herself and then switched on the output meter at its lowest current. She could feel her body throbbing and trembling in every nerve and fibre as the stored up energy passed into her. It produced almost instantly a feeling of extreme elation, of exhilaration, and of vast well being.

It was like a heady wine yet possessing none of the after effects. The current she was absorbing now would mingle with her own energy and restore to her much of the vigour and freshness of youth of which the years had inevitably robbed her. In no way could this energy make her appear again as a girl in her teens—but it did mean that she would apparently remain at her present age for as many years as she chose.

At length she was satisfied with the amount of current that she had given herself and switched the machine off.

Before leaving it, however, she removed from it one of the most vital connecting bars so that by no possible means could any of the other members of the ship, if their suspicions carried them that far, cause the energy to be lost.

This done, she left the laboratory and quietly made her way to the control room. She entered amid a sombre silence to find the men and women gathered about their silent dead children who were now on the main table covered with one enormous sheet. There seemed to be some kind of religious service in progress, one of the men with an open Bible on his outspread palm. At Merva's entry there was a general glance in her direction. She withstood the scrutiny of the eyes with complete calm and came forward, her raven-haired head held high.

"For the purposes of Christian burial," the man with the Bible said, glancing in Merva's direction, "do you desire that Rigilus shall be included in this ceremony?"

"I have already attended to that," Merva answered. "What I would like is to be present at the actual ejection of these unfortunate offspring of yours into space."

"We are not inclined to regard that request with any favour," the man with the Bible answered.

Merva hesitated, feeling at last that she was unable to withstand the cold stares that were fixed upon her. She set her lips, turned and left the lounge without another word.

CHAPTER FOUR

PLAN FOR REVENGE

MERVA was deeply asleep when something suddenly awakened her. Immediately she sat up in the bed, her hand feeling quickly for the ray gun she always left on the table beside her. Just for the moment she wondered if it was Exodus who had awakened her by some movement or other, for he slept in a bed not very far away from her in the same compartment, but almost instantly she realised that this was not the case.

Around her bed, their grim faces illumined by the everlasting stars, were four women. Despite the dimness of the light Merva knew them well enough to almost instantly recognize their features. They were four of the women whose children had died.

"Well," Merva demanded, her emotions as usual held under admirable control, "what is it that you want?"

"The truth," one of the women answered grimly. "Get out of that bed, Merva, immediately!"

"I will do nothing of the sort!"

The four women did not waste any more time. Before she had the chance to grasp what was happening Merva found herself seized by arms and legs and dragged out onto the floor. Swift movements, obviously planned beforehand, made it that before she could put up any kind of trouble to save herself she was bound hand and foot and then dragged to her feet. Breathing hard, her black hair tumbling over her face, she struggled desperately to free herself.

"I shouldn't waste your time if I were you," said the woman who had first spoken. "We know how to tie knots and we know how to get at the truth when we want it, and what is more, we're going to. Aboard this ship there is no form of accepted law or justice—therefore it becomes essential that we take the law into our own hands.

"You're going to be asked quite a few questions, Merva, and if you don't answer them the way we think you should you will be made to."

"Questions," Merva exclaimed, furiously, tossing her hair from her eyes. "What kind of questions? I have nothing to say!"

"That is a matter of opinion."

Again before she could do anything about it Merva was seized between the four women and, struggling frantically, was carried from the room and along to the lounge. None of the men were present: evidently this was a move decided upon by the women alone so it was quite possible that the men knew exactly what was happening. Possibly, too, they felt that a better effect could be gained if they kept out of it.

"We are not satisfied," the spokeswoman said, "that the death of our children was brought about in the way you suggested, therefore we mean to find out the truth. It is possible that, cold and hard natured though you are, you still have enough motherly instinct to protect your own. At any rate that remains to be seen. Fetch Exodus," the woman added briefly, and immediately two of her colleagues left the lounge.

Merva, lying upon the floor and still struggling uselessly to break the cords around her wrists and ankles, glared up in fury. She knew she could expect no mercy whatever from her own sex, that the wiles that she might use upon a man and perhaps melt the most ruthless of his intentions were utterly useless here. For this reason she felt fear though she struggled desperately not to show it.

"What do you want with Exodus?" she demanded.

"You'll see," said the spokeswoman, dispassionately. Presently Exodus was led into the room, still in his sleeping clothes, and he looked at his mother in vague wonder as she lay upon the floor and then he glanced at the faces around him.

"The issue, Merva," said the spokeswoman, "is perfectly simple. We believe our children died through some machination of yours. Whether they were killed deliberately from sheer hatred or whether you had some particular reason for using them before they died we have no means of knowing. But we do intend to find out if you were the instigator of the tragedy. At the moment Exodus is the only child left aboard the ship. Unless you tell us the truth, there will be no children left aboard the ship five minutes from now."

"What!"

Merva jerked herself up on to one elbow and looked around her fearfully. "You can't mean that you're going to kill Exodus for absolutely no reason at all!"

"We shall kill Exodus unless you tell us the truth," the spokeswoman replied. "We realise that it is not exactly fair to Exodus—but it is a case of the sins of the fathers, or mothers, in this case—being visited upon the children, but we mean to get at the truth even if we have to commit murder to do so. You can prevent that by telling us what we wish to know."

"I have already told you the truth," Merva declared desperately.

"First," the spokeswoman said, "before the ultimate necessity of destroying Exodus, we can perhaps make you talk by a little gentle persuasion. It all depends on whether you are strong enough to resist our methods."

"There is nothing you fools can do that will intimidate me," Merva retorted.

None of the women answered that, instead, the one who I had been doing all the talking took a sharply pointed instrument from her pocket. At first glance it looked rather like a carpenter's awl or else an extremely sharp darning needle driven into a big handle. Holding it significantly in front of her the woman gave an icy smile.

"You have a very beautiful face, Merva—at least I will say that for you—but after a little treatment with this instrument your beauty will be there no more. This is not the simple needle-like instrument that it appears to be: it is a surgical probe, the point covered with an indelible dye.

"The dye is non-poisonous but it nevertheless enters into the pigment of the skin. It will be quite possible to mottle your face in such a way that every man in the ship will turn from you with loathing, and you yourself will finally destroy every mirror into which you happen to gaze. Which do you prefer? That I use this instrument upon you, or destroy your son?"

Merva writhed desperately upon the floor. A fine glaze of perspiration had appeared upon her face, and seeing it, the other women looked at each other and nodded significantly. At last, for the first time, Merva was afraid.

"Very well," the spokeswoman said at last, shrugging, "since you do not see fit to talk, you compel me to act."

With that she seized Merva's black hair in a relentless grip and forced her head back savagely. Merva gave a little gasp of pain but the spokeswoman took no notice. She was by far the strongest of the four women and since Merva was so tightly bound she could do nothing to prevent the iron grip on her hair exposing her face to the needlepoint of the weapon of torture.

"You have one more chance," the spokeswoman said.

To Merva the entire view was limited to the intense thinness of the instrument's point poised directly in front of her face. She breathed hard and struggled in vain.

"Wait," she panted breathlessly, "wait a moment. There is no need for this descent into barbarism. I will tell you what you want to know."

The spokeswoman hesitated as though uncertain whether to accept Merva's word or not. Finally she relaxed and stood up looking down on the sprawling Merva, the rest of the women standing with their arms folded, waiting.

"The death of your children was the work of Rigilus, although the original idea was mine," Merva lied. "What I was endeavouring to do, and which would also have been a surprise to you, was to give them eternal life so that they would be better able to withstand this awful journey and even survive at the end of it. Something went wrong with the apparatus and Rigilus and your children were all killed. That is the truth: I swear it is!"

The women looked at one another and finally the spokeswoman seemed to make up her mind and, stooping, she began to undo the cords fastened about Merva's wrists and ankles. Merva made no move while this activity was in progress and when she finally struggled to her feet she looked across towards her son.

"I take it then," she asked, glancing about her, "that you have decided to accept my word?"

"The situation is far from satisfactory," the spokeswoman answered curtly, "but for the moment we are compelled to accept your word for there is no other evidence to the contrary. That does not mean, however, that we have decided to accept the situation as it is. Since we have little else to occupy us for the rest of our lives we shall spend a great deal of time determining what did happen with that apparatus in the laboratory. Fortunately we know which one it is and we shall also take the necessary steps to prevent you doing anything to destroy it."

"Which is as good as saying that you do *not* accept my word?" Merva demanded.

"That is correct," the spokeswoman answered coldly.

Merva gave a bitter glance, adjusted the zip fasteners on her disarranged and exceedingly ornate pyjama suit and then turned to leave the lounge, catching at Exodus' shoulder as she went. The child gave her a bewildered glance as he found himself impelled roughly into the corridor. Without pause Merva hurried along to the laboratory instead of her bedroom, bundling the child along beside her. Only when she had reached the laboratory and dosed the door did she release him.

"Stand over there," she ordered, "I have an important job to do."

The child obeyed, wandering sleepily into a distant corner Merva's eyes following him, then she turned and picked up a curiously fashioned instrument from a bench nearby.

In appearance it was not unlike an old-fashioned blowlamp except that the nozzle was over a foot long. Here was yet another of the devices which she had completed during the recent months.

Operating a control switch she directed the nozzle at the nearby tube chair that was screwed down to the floor. The moment she pressed the switch on her instrument the chair became mysteriously hazed with a lavender glow, after which it swiftly turned green and then with a sudden back draught of evil smelling vapours it entirely disappeared leaving behind nothing but a slowly dispersing haze of acrid smoke. Exodus from his comer stared blankly, realizing, albeit dimly, that he had just witnessed something of staggering power. His mother, for her part, with a twisted smile, came across to him carrying the deadly weapon in her hand.

"Your mother has a lot of enemies, Exodus," she said slowly, laying her free hand on his shoulder, "and because it is never healthy to have enemies I intend to destroy them. I have taught you a good deal about electronics even at your young age and you may have understood something of what I have told you. See therefore if you can understand this: heat produces an accelerated vibration of the fabric of space, which is interpreted by the physical senses as heat. All that this instrument does is to electrically agitate the space around a particular object with the result that a stupendous heat is produced, resulting finally in complete collapse of the object concerned, by reason of the fact that its atomic constitution is so agitated it can no longer pull together and finally dissipates.... Now that is a very big worded explanation for a child as young as you but you may be able to grasp part of it. As you grow older I will explain it to you again and again until you finally understand every detail. Now you stay here; your mother has work to do."

Turning, Merva left the laboratory swiftly and then went silently down the corridor outside. As she had expected when she came to peer into the lounge the womenfolk were still there, but now they were augmented by their particular husbands. All of them were standing in a ragged circle conversing, and from their grim faces Merva judged that they were probably discussing her. She gave again that insolently confident smile to herself and levelled her weapon steadily. Without making a sound she entered the big room and the group turned in some surprise. The moment they saw the weapon she was carrying and the expression of diabolical hatred on her marble white face they stepped back very slightly.

"You do well to retreat," Merva remarked, bitterly, "and remember that *I* am confronting you single handed. When you attacked me there were four of you against which I had no chance: now the positions are reversed.

"So you think," she continued, moving forward deliberately with her weapon still at the ready, "that you'll spend all your time hereon investigating the mysteries of the laboratories, do you? Studying how the life energy equipment operates, and if it doesn't do exactly as you think it should you intend to confront me once again with the charge of murdering your children. What kind of a fool do you think I am?"

"We never did think you were a fool," one of the men answered; "indeed, quite the opposite. That's just the trouble."

"A little while ago," Merva said, still advancing steadily, "you asked me to tell the truth as to what happened to your children. I did not tell the truth but I am doing so now. Each and every one of them gave his or her life energy and it was stored in that scientific equipment in the laboratory. They gave their life energy because I have decided to live a thousand years and still be as young when this colossal journey has ended as I am now—young enough to be able to fashion the great scheme of vengeance that Rigilus originally conceived. So you see, whether you like it or not, your children have given everything to the plan of revenge whilst you, their parents, have given nothing. You refused to fall in with Rigilus's commands and he was compelled to bow to your wishes because of your superior numbers. I do not intend to bow to your wishes under any circumstances nor do I intend to allow you to pry and probe with the final intention of accusing me of murder. What I do intend to do is eliminate each and every one of you, even as your children and Rigilus himself were eliminated.

"There are only two people who matter in the Universe to me. Myself and my son. Into him I shall inject the poison of revenge for the day when he and I shall stand side by side, a thousand years hence, mistress and master of a plan which not only will overwhelm the Earth but the whole Solar System."

"Madness," one of the men muttered, "that's what it is, madness!"

"Yes, perhaps it is," Merva admitted, shrugging, "I make no apology for that. I have the one saving grace of knowing exactly what I want, and what is more I know how to get it."

In that instant she ceased talking and pressed the button upon her weapon. Immediately the men and women forming the circle endeavoured to fling themselves to one side, but they were not quick enough to escape the devastating area of the vibration.

Merva kept her finger relentlessly pressed upon the weapon's button and when she left the lounge five minutes later there was nothing to show for her activities but a haze of dispersing, evil smelling smoke.

And the vessel sped on....

* * * *

The situation was at last as Merva wanted it. She was completely rid of all her enemies and free to plan the future exactly as she wished. There was, of course, no doubt in her mind as to what she intended to do—she would use the energy derived from the children to give herself and her son a thousand years of life. By that time she would have evolved the perfect plan and no doubt have discovered a way to drive the mighty space liner back across the course it had already taken but at an infinitely greater speed than upon its outward journey.

She would not even have the loneliness of space to weigh her down for with her son there was always the assurance of company, nor was it company that could pall for she had so much to teach him; he had so much to ask her that there would be very little time for idle moments. Yes, the situation was perfect and, not in the least disturbed by her conscience after the elimination of the men and women in the lounge, Merva picked up Exodus from the laboratory and calmly returned to her apartment to catch up on a good deal of lost sleep.

She awakened again to the awareness of strange sounds |coming from a far distant quarter of the ship. They were not loud enough to have actually awakened her for she felt refreshed after many hours of deep sleep, therefore for the moment the puzzle was complete. She glanced towards Exodus' bed, thinking that perhaps he was responsible for the noises, but to her surprise he was comfortably stretched out, sleeping deeply.

Puzzled and even slightly afraid, Merva slipped out quickly from the bed, drew her wrap about her and hurried down the corridor to the source of the noises. They appeared to be coming from the immense storage hold in which were kept the vast quantities of supplies necessary for this stupendous journey.

The noise sounded like someone hammering on the huge metal door. Just for an instant as she stood there alone in the corridor, knowing that she was in the depths of interstellar space, and with only a young and quite helpless boy for company, Merva felt her flesh creep a little. What conceivably could be alive on this spaceship when she knew that she had destroyed the last of her foes?

It took every vestige of her courage to slide away the massive bar that held the door in place and then open the door slowly and peer into the gloom beyond. Her hand felt round fumblingly for the light switch and snapped it on. At the sight that met her she caught her breath in a tremendous gasp of amazement.

There in the bright light stood the six children whom she had imagined were dead and already ejected from the space machine!

Instantly they came hurrying around her, full of that complete trust which is the prerogative of a child. Merva stared at them in bewilderment, trying to fathom how it was that they came to be alive when she had seen them not so very long ago upon the table in the lounge covered with a sheet. But she had not been present at the intended ejection of their bodies into outer space. She remembered how bluntly she had been told that her presence would not be welcome at such a ceremony.... What then had happened to so change the circumstances?

She said nothing there and then but ushered the children along the corridor into the lounge, studying them intently as she followed behind them. They appeared to be in perfect health again and from the way they moved there was obviously no lack of energy either.

Smiling to herself, Merva followed them into the lounge and then after insistent clamourings she concocted a story to explain the disappearance of their parents. She explained it away by saying that they had all been expelled out into space when the window of the room they were in had been struck and destroyed by a meteor, and the air had rushed out in the void. At their young age the children readily accepted the lie, along with her reassurance that she had repaired the breached hull, and that the cosmic accident was unlikely to ever happen again.

She finally left them and went out to prepare a meal for each one of them. As they ate it with an avidity that astonished her she questioned each one of them in turn and eventually managed to piece together what was evidently the truth.

Closer examination had revealed to their parents that they were not dead but stunned into something very close to what might be called suspended animation by the tremendous shock of having their bodily energy drained from them. Apparently their heartbeats had dropped almost to zero but a very careful analysis had shown that the heartbeats were still there and therefore they were alive.

They had been put in the storage hold for a reason that none of them seemed to understand but which Merva grasped readily enough. Evidently their parents had been planning some kind of scheme that they had intended later to spring upon her—Merva. It was the realisation of this fact that made her all the more satisfied that she had taken the right step in eliminating the adults completely. She bolstered her story by telling the children that their parents had known of the impending meteor strike and had placed the children in the storage hold for their own safety.

She was now left her with their progeny to mould and train exactly as she wished alongside Exodus.

Far from resenting the reappearance of the children Merva accepted it gladly. It gave her three girls and four boys, including her own son, who, when they matured would be capable of producing progeny and that perhaps would be the beginning of a small but relentless army who would exact the vengeance which she had in mind.

It meant that her original plan which was to include only herself and her son would have to undergo revision: not that that mattered, for the more there were to carry out the plan the better.

So from that moment onwards she appointed herself as the children's mentor and day by day and week by week taught them all the arts of scientific accomplishment as she knew them together with the doctrine of revenge that was always uppermost in her thoughts. Cleverly, she blamed the death of their parents directly on the Earth authorities, who had been responsible for unjustly banishing them into space. Inevitably the children were moulded by what she taught and told them, and deprived of their own parents they accepted everything she said as being the absolute truth. Out here in the depths of space there were no other adults, no other minds, to give the lie to anything which Merva said.

Inevitably she was the absolute controller of the ship.

The only thing which she did particularly notice was the slow change in Exodus as month by month and presently year by year he moved onwards towards maturity.

In the early stages he had seemed to be an absolute replica of herself, but gradually there came a slow transition of his mental outlook and it was forced upon Merva that he had a great deal of his father in him. Not only in physical appearance, for very early on he revealed his late father's majesty of bearing and insolence of expression, but in his mental outlook as well. He had all of Rigilus' manner allied to his mother's complete ruthlessness and the two together were a decidedly formidable combination.

It was not very long before Merva realised that she had a problem child on her hands insofar as he only obeyed her orders when he felt that they would be of any particular benefit to him, and outside of that he was completely defiant, nor could anything that she could do cause him to change his policy.

The one advantage so far as Merva could see was, that being the type of boy he was, Exodus assumed complete domination over the other children and they, being of much weaker stock, accepted his leadership without question. Perhaps in the end, Merva considered, this might prove to be an advantage.

For her, the weeks and months spread gradually into years and the awful journey still continued uninterrupted, the vessel now being apparently billions of miles from the nearest point of contact. There was nothing now but the stars and the far distant Milky Way galaxy and the nebulae beyond that. Of Earth, the Solar System and its Sun there was no longer the slightest trace.

Years—years—years. Merva did not appear to be a day older, so completely did the life energy she had absorbed at regular intervals maintained her age at one constant level. But Exodus was now fifteen and the children around him between that age and twelve. Everyone of them was well educated and with a highly scientific outlook— Merva had seen to that—and likewise every one of them was concentrated upon the one thing nearest to her own heart, revenge upon the descendants of the people of Earth for the injustice which they had brought into being.

Not that Merva had confined herself exclusively to the education of the children. She had found time here and there to concentrate her coldly scientific brain upon the problem of devising weapons with which to wage destruction upon Earthlings when the time came.

So far the weapons had not got beyond the drawing board stage; she planned at a later date, when the children were far more mature than they were now, that they should all work upon the task of making the weapons for themselves, thereby understanding in most complete detail what exactly was required from each one of them. Her plan was to make each boy and each girl, when they became men and women, the controller of one particular weapon and a specialist in his or her line. In this way she felt confident that there could be no mistakes when the far distant day came for the onslaught to be waged.

She knew perfectly well of course that the only two survivors of the thousand year voyage would be herself and her son but she was relying a good deal on the mechanism of hereditary for the other children when grown to adult life, to hand on to their own children all the knowledge which they had absorbed, most of it naturally inherited and the rest of it taught. Hence her reason for being so completely thorough with every detail of each weapon.

"To you, Exodus," she said on one occasion, when he had reached the age of eighteen, "I am handing over this automatic annihilator. You will find after careful study of the details that it is by far the most powerful weapon ever conceived. Operating on full power it will be capable of blotting out an entire city with one blow and I very much doubt if the peoples of Earth, unprepared for an onslaught, will be able to counteract anything of that nature. That is the main thing that we have in our favour, Exodus—the absolute surprise with which we shall attack."

Exodus nodded slowly as his mother looked at him with her earnest green eyes, her face set as ever in that cruel, inflexible mould.

"Are you quite sure, mother, that you are not taking too much for granted?" he asked after a while.

"That sounds to me rather a ridiculous question, Exodus, since I never take anything for granted. What exactly do you mean?"

"It is not that I fear our inability to finish the journey," he said, pondering. "The only thing I am wondering about is shall we have enough power to make the journey back—and even more shall we have enough ingenuity to be able to work out how to get back to Earth within a reasonable time? You say the journey outwards before the switchboard is released from the electronic brain will take a thousand years. If it were to take us that long to get back I cannot help but feel that the tedium of the trip would bring both you and I to the point of looking for suicide as a way to end it."

Merva looked at her son fixedly.

"How very much like your father you are," she said slowly. "He once said something like that, though not in quite so many words. I'm going to say to you what I said to him—a statement like that is nothing else but sheer defeatism! You don't suppose all the energy, learning and struggle which is being gone through in these years is going to be terminated by anything as ridiculous as suicide, do you?"

"Naturally I don't wish it to," Exodus shrugged, "I'm merely stating what appears to me as a problem. What methods are we going to use to return at a speed faster than we have made the outward journey?"

Merva looked irritated. "Yon need not have the slightest fear that we shall find our way back and quickly too. Remember that this ship is not moving at anything like its optimum velocity. Once the locks of the controls on the switchboard are removed it will be possible to increase the speed very close to the speed of light—186,000 miles per second. We shall do this by accelerating constantly. We can do this because the atomic energy basis of our engines is almost inexhaustible. Travelling at the speed of light, our ship could reach Earth on the return trip from Alpha Centauri in just a little over four years. Of course that is impossible, because we will need time to build up the speed, and then an equal amount of time to decelerate at the other end. But clearly we can reach the Earth in a comparatively reasonable time and then strike."

Exodus nodded but did not comment, a fact that made Merva wonder what exactly had passed through his mind at that moment.

"I assume then," he said presently, "that you are now going to teach me all there is to know about this atomic annihilator."

"Exactly," Merva assented, "just you alone. The others will be taught how to operate the other instruments in the hope that they will hand it on to their children later—and incidentally Exodus, you are in your nineteenth year and therefore more than mature. Have you singled out amongst the girls there are in this space machine which one you have decided upon?"

"I have," he answered calmly.

"And has she responded to your attentions or has she some particular desire for one of the other young men?"

"It doesn't concern me what particular desires she has," Exodus replied. "*I* have decided which one it is to be and I shall take her whether she likes it or not."

Merva nodded slowly and then gave a rather grim smile.

"There is little doubt as to whose child you are," she said gravely. "Very well, Exodus, I'll leave that particular matter entirely in your hands. I would point out to you that the need for more children is becoming somewhat urgent. Take a look at the gauge on the life energy machine there."

Exodus crossed to it and studied its complicated meter system then he turned with a look of surprise.

"How does it happen that such a lot of energy has been used up?" he questioned. "I understood you to say when you explained about this machine that there was enough energy to last a thousand years—that you would have all you need, including myself, of course."

"I miscalculated somewhat," Merva sighed. "Not that it signifies for there will be other children from whom energy can be taken. Up to now you have not had any of the energy, because had you done so it would have necessitated you staying apparently at the particular age at which you received the energy. That would have been absurd had you remained somewhere round a constant twelve years of age; there would have been no point in it, but now that you are in your nineteenth year the first absorption of energy can begin. Hence the necessity for children because once you and I are both using the energy there is bound to be a very big drain upon the supply we have here."

"Suppose," Exodus said, again with that thoughtful look upon his powerfully cut face, "we ever arrive at the point where there is only enough energy for either you or I. What would be done in a case like that?"

Merva sighed. "What a boy you are for anticipating trouble." There is no conceivable reason why there shouldn't always be enough energy for both of us providing we can maintain a constant supply of children which just makes it that the energy seems to last just from generation to generation. If however we did get into the desperate position of having to choose between one and the other I would of course choose to perpetuate myself because I know more than all of you put together."

A slight gleam seemed to come into Exodus' greenish grey eyes, but he did not make any further comment. Instead he said:

"When you are ready to show me the details of the atomic annihilator mother, I am ready to listen. Then when I have had the first lesson I shall go in search of Vilnia and tell her that in accordance with your wishes I have decided to marry her."

"So you intend to thrust the responsibility of your marriage to Vilnia upon me? That it?"

"Certainly, just in case she should register some kind of protest. It is always comforting to have someone in authority to fall back upon if there should be any kind of argument."

Merva nodded, but there was a frown upon her brow. She was not altogether sure that she liked the situation. She knew perfectly well that Exodus was quite capable of looking after himself and had never needed anybody upon which to fall back. What he was actually doing was exhibiting a great deal of his mother's subtlety insofar that when it came to a matter of extreme delicacy he did not intend to take the responsibility if he could thrust it elsewhere.

"Take up your position before the annihilator," Merva ordered. "I'll show you what has to be done."

Exodus obeyed and for the next two hours he was absorbed in the most profound concentration as his mother gave him every detail that she herself had conceived concerning the diabolically effective instrument.

Merva could not be sure whether his profound interest in the invention was out of respect for her erudition or if it was that he wanted to get every detail at his finger ends for his personal use. She endeavoured to convince herself that this desire on his part was purely to further the great scheme of vengeance that she had so constantly expounded.

She would not and could not believe that he was perhaps learning everything possible so that should the time come, he could if necessary take her place....

In a word, Merva was faced by something that made her profoundly uncomfortable—a son whom she felt she could not trust.

CHAPTER FIVE

TREACHERY

ONCE this first lesson was over Exodus did not linger in the laboratory; instead he took a cool but respectful leave of his mother then hurried through the depths of the ship until he came into the lounge. Here he looked around him quickly on the young teenagers, his eyes searching for Vilnia. Failing to find her he went further and finally tracked her down in the enormous conning tower in the summit of the vessel where she was seated on the padded ledge under the great dome, her eyes turned to the frigid glitter of the stars.

"I have been looking for you, Vilnia," Exodus said, coming forward.

At the sound of his voice Vilnia turned quickly towards him. She was a slim, blonde, elfin girl only just on the edge of maturity. She had wide blue eyes that looked as though she were incessantly wondering what had brought about the incredible state of affairs in that she and her contemporaries were forever condemned to remain in this speeding space machine.

"Looking for me?" she repeated as Exodus came up and settled beside her on the padded seat. "Why, does somebody want me?"

"Yes." Exodus gave a calm nod. "I do. I have just returned from a long conversation with my mother," he explained. "She has decreed that the time has come for marriage between each of us aboard this vessel—a matter far more important than it would be in the normal society of a planet—so I decided to seek you out and tell you that I have decided to marry you."

"From the way you speak it does not appear that I am allowed much choice," Vilnia said, rather coldly. "For your information, Exodus—or do you know already—my affection is entirely for Drando, and I do think—"

"We are not interested in Drando," Exodus interrupted. "I said that *I* have decided to marry you and that precludes the possibility of anybody else even attempting it. Where your personal inclinations lie does not matter. As I said before we are not on a planet where there is a matter of choice and for the same reason affection does not enter it either.

"I realise that we are both only young as yet even though my mother tells me that I am mature far beyond my years, but there is a certain reason why the matter of marriage cannot be delayed by any of us much longer. Needless to say the reason is entirely scientific "

Vilnia turned away from his direct, dominating gaze and instead once more surveyed the heavens. There was a certain droop about her slim, still somewhat undeveloped shoulders.

"Even though we are not on a planet, Exodus," she said, after a moment or two, "there are still certain basic human emotions that need to be satisfied. At least I think so. Nothing but desperate unhappiness can come from a marriage which has no more feeling or warmth than those stars out there."

"Which means," Exodus commented, "that you are reducing marriage to the old formula of sentimentality and love under which disguise the demands of lust are satisfied."

The girl looked at him sharply, astonished. He seemed quite unmoved by her glance and continued:

"My mother has taught me—and I believe implicitly in everything she has to say—that to the true scientist love and sentiment are outworn emotions. One marries for only one definite reason—the production of progeny Those progeny are not just produced for the sake of it but again for another definite reason and in this case a scientific one, so you see the whole thing is really little more than a straightforward business deal and human feelings does not even come into it.

"I have singled you out in particular as opposed to the other two girls because you seem the most intelligent. The matter of your physical attraction does not enter into it. Since it is essential that the children of our union should be as intelligent and if possible more intelligent than we are it becomes imperative that I seek the girl who is best suited for that purpose. That is what I have decided, Vilnia, and you have no alternative but to fall in with that decision."

The girl rose from the padded seat and looked down on Exodus steadily.

"You have assumed a great deal, Exodus, and of course I respect you insofar as you are endeavouring to fulfil the wishes of your mother, but it so happens that I have an individuality of my own and not for one moment would I consider union with you. I have already told you that Drando is my choice and indeed we have almost made up our minds to complete the bargain. Anything that you can say, even though you are the son of our ruler, cannot make the slightest difference."

Exodus shrugged. "In that case you had better advise my mother of your decision but I do not think she will take very kindly to it either."

"Your mother," Vilnia said. deliberately, "has no right to control our lives."

"That is a matter of opinion. If somebody does not control our lives what kind of a chaos are we going to get into? I wouldn't advise you to inform my mother of your rejection of my proposal, Vilnia, because if you do she is quite liable to seek another of the men as a husband for you and I can assure you it would not be Drando."

Vilnia was silent, recalling the other young men of the party and inwardly shuddering to herself. She could not tolerate any of them and if it came to it union with them would be worse than marriage to Exodus.

Exodus rose, his big hand resting on her shoulder.

"I am sorry, Vilnia, if I seem callous in the way I treat this most delicate of matters but I cannot help the way I am made. My mother is the ruler and my father was the ruler before her so it is not unnatural that I have that same dominating strain. All I ask is that you have the sense to realise that a great honour is being conferred upon you."

"That I do realise," Vilnia responded, "but it still does not make me anxious to have you. I shall tell your mother exactly how the situation stands and see what she has to say."

Exodus did not respond. He watched Vilnia leave the conning tower with graceful movements and finally dis. appear through the doorway that led to the main corridor. Musing to himself he sat down again and contemplated the interminable wastes of space, his eyes settling at length on the still incredibly distant spot of light which marked the position of Alpha Centauri. At this enormous distance he could not tell that Proxima Centauri lay close beside the parent star, Alpha being of course a dual sun.

Thus engaged he completely lost himself in speculations that were of remarkable depth considering that as yet he was only a young man in his nineteenth year. But then the education he had received and the circumstances in which he had lived from the very moment of his birth had done much to bring maturity to him many years ahead of time....

It was the return of Vilnia that finally aroused him. She advanced slowly from the doorway, her elfin face white and pinched as though she had gazed upon some kind of phantom. Exodus recognised the signs and gave a rather taut smile as he rose to his feet.

"I gather," he said, quietly, "that you have seen my mother?"

"Yes." Vilnia's voice was low. "She told me that if I do not agree to your proposal I shall be compelled to marry Hazalet. That I will not do under any circumstances. He is unintelligent, boorish and hasn't the least idea how to treat a woman. You, Exodus, at least have intelligence...."

"Thank you," Exodus responded gravely. "I hope also that I know how to treat a woman. Do not imagine that because I have been so matter-of-fact about this proposal I shall treat you as though you are less than the dust, Vilnia—but on the other hand, you can't expect me to be romantic because I am simply not made that way."

Exodus could not be expected to know that his father had used almost those self same words so long before when he had fallen under the spell of Merva. In this case the situation was reversed and Vilnia inclined her fair head as Exodus laid a large and possessive hand up her shoulder....

And the ship sped on.

A week later, not only the marriage of Vilnia and Exodus took place but also the marriages of all the young men and women aboard the vessel. Merva was insistent upon it and herself as commander of the vessel performed the necessary ceremony. She wondered even as she performed it why such a technicality was necessary since all normal conventions and regulations had long since gone by the board. She could only assume that she did it because ingrained deep within her and indeed in the participants of the marriages were the instincts that demanded the observance of age-old customs.

Surveying the young couples, the great windows behind them carrying their eternal picture of the stars, Merva gave her slow, cynical smile.

"It is not my place to tell you what you shall do or what you shall not do," she said, deliberately, "but this much I feel you should know. All of us here are dedicated to the cause of ultimate vengeance and it is essential to the perfection of that plan that I as your leader should survive the thousand years necessary to bring that plan to fruition. That can only be accomplished through the presence of children and that obviously is where you come in.

"It is now no longer a secret from you that your children are used for life energy even as you were when children and by that means I am permitted to continue living through the endless years, never growing older and able to be your guide, mentor and friend."

Nobody said anything but Exodus gave a faintly cynical smile that his mother immediately noted. She glanced in his direction.

"Did I say something particularly amusing, Exodus?" she questioned, coldly.

"Not that I am aware of," he answered with complete calm. "One can surely be permitted a passing thought which brings a smile to the face? I feel, mother, that it is that particular virtue in which you have failed. You see no humour in any situation, but I fortunately do. Without it I should consider our existence a very grave business indeed."

"Your father often smiled," Merva snapped, "and always in the wrong places. However, to resume my observations—the continuity of the little society that we have built up here in space depends entirely upon me and ultimately upon you. I shall expect you to do your duty as husbands and wives...."

With that she turned away and walked majestically from the lounge where the ceremony had been conducted. The various couples broke up and Exodus finally found himself looking at Vilnia steadily. Her eyes dropped under the intensity of his gaze.

"Which of us is it that you fear most, Vilnia, my mother or me?"

"Your mother, naturally," Vilnia responded, promptly. "Even when she is not present one can feel that she is watching from somewhere, probably by scientific instruments following our every move, dictating everything that we must do and always hinting what must be the penalty if we do not do what she has proposed.

"I can understand you tolerating it, Exodus, because after all she is your mother, but to me she means nothing; she simply exists as a complete tyrant who will never die. She will always be present even after I and all these others have gone. You I do not fear even though I do not love you. For one thing you are almost my own age and to a certain extent we have views in common even if there is no romantic interchange."

"You do not suppose, do you, that I will be forever dominated by my mother?" Exodus asked.

"I fail to see how you can avoid it."

"In time, Vilnia, you will learn. Mother has taught me the art of domination and revenge to the exclusion of all else and for that reason I feel there must come a time when...."

Exodus paused, shaking his head, and Vilnia looked at him quickly.

"You don't mean to say that you are planning something against your mother?"

"It is too early yet to say *what* I am planning and in any case the nebulous scheme which I have in mind may take many years to evolve—but come, we have no more time to waste. We have to get dressed in readiness for the celebration dinner which mother has insisted must be given."

* * * *

The following 'day' Merva was somewhat surprised to behold Vilnia entering the comfortably furnished apartment, which represented the headquarters. The girl was looking half frightened yet resolute as she advanced quickly towards the broad table where Merva was at work. As usual, plans for scientific instruments and weapons of destruction were absorbing her but she ceased her concentrations as the girl stood before her, waiting.

"Well," Merva asked, with a rather forced smile, "and what has my new daughter to say to me?"

"It is because I am your new daughter that I feel in a rather vague way that I am responsible for your safety."

"My *safety*?" Merva's eyebrows rose in surprise. "Well, much as I appreciate your solicitude, Vilnia, I can assure you that I am perfectly capable of looking after myself."

"In the normal way, yes, but this is something different. I don't know whether it really signifies but I think it just as well to warn you that in a conversation I had with Exodus yesterday he hinted at the fact that he would not always be under your domination."

"I see." Merva gave a rather grim smile. "I can assure you, Vilnia, that Exodus has *never* been under my domination. Right from the day he was born he has proved to be a problem child, and now he is rapidly growing to manhood I have even more difficulty in keeping him under control."

Vilnia quickly and then rather nervously added, "I don't exactly mean it in that sense. I felt from the way he talked that he had some dim idea in the back of his mind about getting rid of you. Naturally he didn't tell me anything and he hinted that it would be a long time yet before he acted, but I did think that you ought to have the facts."

"You do not mean," Merva asked deliberately, "that he spoke of taking my life?"

"No, not exactly that, but…." Vilnia hesitated obviously unsure how to continue; for she could not say that she was giving this warning through any love for Merva, but because she felt that it might place her in a better light as far as her mother-in-law was concerned.

"I find all this very hard to believe, Vilnia," Merva said at length, "but on the other hand I feel perfectly sure that you would never make such a statement without due reason. Exodus is a boy with many strange ideas, and now that he is a married man he probably has some feeling of resentment towards me in that I am the controller of the ship and not he. However I can assure you that there is very little he can do to usurp my authority, and thank you for telling me Vilnia."

Vilnia smiled, hesitated, then realising that the interview had terminated on this note she turned and left the room. Merva watched the door close, sat brooding for awhile, then gradually her fist clenched on the table before her.

"It begins to look," she muttered to herself, "that the fears that I have had about Exodus for so long are showing signs of being justified. I have known for long enough that he resents my control, so perhaps I cannot do better than heed this child's warning."

It was strange perhaps that it did not occur to Merva that there was any threat against her personally. She saw in Vilnia's warning only an incipient danger to the life energy machine, the one piece of apparatus that could give her constant life and enable her to stay side by side with Exodus as long as need be.

Indeed Merva's entire being was always centred round that life energy machine. She knew only too well that without it functioning perfectly there would come a rapid end not only to her rulership but also to her life, for even at this moment she was living on borrowed time in that the energy she was using to keep her alive was entirely spurious and failure to keep it maintained would result in death much more rapidly than would normally be the case.

Arriving at a final decision she got to her feet, left the room and made her way to the laboratory. In here she locked herself in and then set about the task of rendering the life energy machine entirely useless unless she herself controlled it. This indeed was a precaution which she had always taken up to now but with Exodus knowing so much about the instrument—she feeling that as her son he should know almost as much as she did—the precautions which she had taken to make it foolproof were no longer operative as far as she was concerned. The removal now of the main crystalline bars that carried the current made the equipment as inoperative as a battery without plates.

"And I must remember," she mused, when the job was done, "to always remember to keep these bars to myself except when the equipment is actually in operation. Whatever bright schemes Exodus has in mind, this will completely scotch them."

A sudden knocking on the door made her turn swiftly. She hurried quickly to a nearby metal cabinet, put the bars within it then closed the door and spun the combination lock. This done she crossed over to the laboratory door and opened it. Exodus was outside in the corridor, a look of vague surprise on his face.

"I'm sorry if I am interrupting some experiment or other," he apologized, coming in nonetheless.

"No. I was just pottering about as usual," his mother replied, following him to the centre of the laboratory. "What brings you here,

Exodus? I should have thought that at this time you would have been more absorbed in your wife than in things of science?"

"I am endeavouring," Exodus replied, "to divide my life into two separate compartments. In the one half I place my usual scientific studies and in the other half I place Vilma. I'm surprised that you of all people should have any thoughts of my having romantic leanings towards Vilnia. Believe me I have none. I see her simply as one of those cogs you are always speaking about, in this great machine of revenge which we are endeavouring to build between us."

"I'm glad that you keep that uppermost in your mind," Merva said, "for that is the most essential thing of all."

Exodus shook his head. "I cannot agree there, mother. It seems to me that children and life energy are every bit as important as the scheme of vengeance, therefore Vilnia ranks with equal importance to science. However maybe we are following a pointless argument so I'd better tell you why I really came here."

"By all means."

"I thought you might be interested to know that I have an idea for one of the most powerful weapons ever conceived."

Merva smiled in the way that one does when tolerating someone many years younger.

"It is something," Exodus continued, with a far away look in his eyes, "that embodies a principle certainly not used by you in any of your inventions so far. Without wishing to ridicule anything which you have done I would say that my conception is far more effective than anything you have conceived."

"No matter what it may be so long as it contributes to the eventual destruction of the successors of Earth people."

"I am more than willing to hear all about it," Merva responded. "What kind of an invention is it?"

"It is based on cosmic energy. In this vessel of ours we are completely surrounded by it as a mere glance at the occiligraph shows in a moment. For a long time now I have been pondering how that enormous mass of energy might be used to advantage and at last I think I have a wonderful theory. You would care to hear about it?"

"By all means," Merva nodded, seating herself on a nearby chair.

"Very well then. I see it like this...."

And Exodus began pacing slowly around his thumbs latched in the belt about the waist of his tunic. It was almost impossible for Merva to realise that he was as yet only eighteen: he had all the assurance and the perspicacity of a man twenty years his senior. "Cosmic energy is the most destructive force in the universe, as we well know. Insofar that it has more power than X-rays, gamma-rays, beta or alpha and in its undiluted form—which is to say unshielded either by an atmospheric envelope or electrical fields or even plain lead—it is certain death to living tissue. Expose living tissue for only a few seconds to pure cosmic energy and that tissue is totally destroyed and reduced to dust; Am I not right?"

"Definitely so," Merva agreed, completely attentive. "I tried a long time ago to make some use of cosmic energy but unfortunately my experiments did not get me very far. It is such an unpredictable power with which to tamper. What exactly do you mean to do?"

"I had thought of building an enormous cosmic energy storage plant—by which I mean a plant capable of absorbing cosmic energy in much the same way as your life energy machine over there. In your case of course, energy is absorbed from human beings. In the plant I have in mind the energy of the cosmos which is exactly on the same principle would be absorbed instead and then re-radiated whenever required. Fundamentally the principle of the thing is very much the same as your life energy absorber, the only difference being that we shall deal with cosmic energy instead of life energy. It does seem to me that the two energies have a great deal in common—one is the energy of human beings and the other is the eternal life energy of the cosmos. In fact, it must be, because cosmic radiation is everywhere. You find it as close to the Earth as we find it out here in the deeps of space, and as we shall continue to find it no matter how far we travel.

"Build a plant like that," Exodus continued, a bright gleam in his eyes, "and when that glorious day comes for us to attack the Earth we shall have a generator stored to the limit with cosmic energy which we have gathered together immediately outside the atmosphere of Earth. I do not suggest that we get the energy together while we are such an enormous distance away from our home planet, because that would undoubtedly mean the dissipation of the energy throughout the years as we made the return journey. Cosmic energy being anywhere we can absorb it at any time we choose and wherever we choose providing we are in space. Is that quite clear so far?"

"Yes, it is clear enough," Merva admitted slowly: "the only thing troubling me is the fact that you do not seem to have considered the danger attached to the initial experiments. I am quite prepared to admit that a generator stored with cosmic energy, when complete, would be the mightiest weapon ever contrived, but in the early stages of construction you would have to experiment with cosmic energy almost constantly and since you are flesh and blood the energy might eventually have a very serious effect upon you."

"Pioneers always take the risks," Exodus replied, shrugging. "I have not the least fear but what I shall conduct the experiments in perfect safety and in the fullest insulation—and there is the virtue that I have unnumbered years in which to make my experiments. My point is this, mother," he continued, striding forward until he was facing her directly, "when the day finally comes to strike I wish to have in my possession a weapon so shattering, so completely reliable, that the chance of defeat is entirely ruled out. Effective though the instruments are which you have designed I still do not feel inclined to pin all my faith on them. I want something that at one blow can destroy half the world completely. A weapon that can reduce whole civilisations and whole human beings into complete dust with one fell swoop. Your weapons are ideal for individual picking off as one might call it, or for concentrating on small points that will not come into the main area, but for the initial blast I say let us have cosmic radiation. Under the withering impact of that human beings will shrivel and vanish like ants on a red hot grill!"

"Exodus, I am proud of you," Merva commented, rising to her feet and moving towards him. "You have your father's immense breadth of outlook and my complete lack of sentiment. The combination of the two has produced an ideal avenger. Naturally it goes without saying that I will help you all I can with a plan like this and then we...."

"I don't think I shall need any help," Exodus said thinking. "I am one that must work alone and entirely to my own ideas. I do not mean by that that I am shutting you out from my activities but I do insist on doing this whole construction alone. The machine is to be mine and the power that goes with it is also to be mine. Like you I find it difficult to share power with anybody."

The eyes of mother and son met for a moment and in neither was there the faintest trace of yielding. Possibly the most discomfited was Merva in that she had come to realise at last that her son was possessed of greater scientific intelligence than either herself or her late husband.

"And when do you intend to start the construction of this machine?" she asked presently, moving away.

"I'm in no hurry. I have the drawings to get out first but I thought it would be as well to let you know what I am doing in case you find me busy on the job without a previous explanation. What I have in mind is to turn the main storage room at the far end of the vessel into the site for the generator. The stuff that is already in there can easily be moved into some of the other holds of the ship and that would leave me ample room for construction. If the generator were to be constructed there, filling one quarter of the ship, the feeder lines from it could afterwards be carried to the nose of the vessel and there we have the whole thing beautifully under control. You will be able to estimate for yourself how much cosmic power there will be in a generator occupying a quarter of a ship this size."

"There can never be too much power," Merva replied. "That is the secret of success, be it human power or elemental power."

"Well then, since you have given your blessing...." Exodus crossed over to the life energy machine and stood contemplating it thoughtfully. Merva watched him, her eyes narrowed over a thought.

"Would it do any harm," Exodus asked, "if you switched this machine on for me so that I can once again refresh my mind as to its principles?"

"It is quite impossible to switch it on without there being a dissipation of life energy," Merva answered him. "There is so little of it that I can't afford to lose any either for your sake or mine, so I'm afraid nothing can be done in that direction."

"That," Exodus said, turning and looking at her, "doesn't make sense. It is as simple to switch this machine on in order to see its operation without it dissipating any energy as it is to switch on the power plant of the space ship without having it to actually drive the vessel. Besides I must have it switched on in order to have a better idea of the basic principles which I have in mind."

Merva shook her head. "I cannot help you there, Exodus."

A grim look came into his face; he crossed over to where his mother was standing.

"This doesn't make sense," he declared flatly. "On the one hand you are willing to help me all you can with this invention then the moment I ask you to make the first move in regard to that help, you refuse to do anything. There can't be any reason why you don't want this machine switched on, can there?"

"Are you quite sure," Merva asked, deliberately, "that this cosmic ray theory of yours is absolutely genuine?"

"Genuine?" Exodus stared at her in amazement. "But of course it's genuine! Why should you so suddenly decide to doubt it?"

"I doubt it, Exodus, because it is so closely linked in basis of operation with this life energy machine of mine. I have known for long enough that you would like to know a great deal more about this life energy machine and I'm going to venture to suggest that this cosmic ray theory of yours, entirely nebulous, has been devised so as to make it necessary for you to thoroughly examine this life energy machine as a supposed basis for your own machine. Now that I do not intend to allow."

"And why not?" Exodus asked, completely blank.

"A little while ago, Exodus, you said that you found it difficult to share power with anybody. I too am of the same mind and there is nothing that could give you greater power than to know more about that life energy machine. You could, if you chose, use just enough energy to give yourself just one more injection and then you could dissipate the remainder, leaving me without anything. I dislike saying such a thing about my own son but I believe in an emergency you would do just that."

"Absolutely ridiculous," Exodus declared flatly. "I admit that I don't like sharing power either with you or anybody else but I'm also remembering that you are also my mother, my own flesh and blood. I want to study this life energy machine for no other purpose than to further my own invention. I beg of you to believe that."

"You'll have to find some other way," Merva said, deliberately. "I have no intention of allowing you to examine that machine."

"There is nothing to stop me doing it in your absence."

"Yes, there is. I intend to place an electrical circuit around it, and it will be so arranged that if you touch any part of that machine you will receive a shock sufficient to kill you. Just as you respect me as your own flesh and blood I respect you for the same reason, but in the final analysis one's own life comes first and I do not propose to take any chances with that. Forget all about that machine, Exodus, and work out your own invention entirely from a theoretical basis. I will willingly check it for you and in detail, correcting it where it fails to match up with this life energy machine as its basis."

Exodus was silent for a long moment, obviously quite unable to understand the situation. Even if he had for a moment suspected that Vilnia had said anything to his mother—which indeed he did not— he would never have expected her to take the course of guarding the life energy machine: rather he would have expected that she would have protected herself. So the puzzle for him was complete.

"Since that is your attitude, mother," he said, briefly, "you leave me no other course than to make the necessary drawings and then submit them to you, and I must say I am not particularly happy over your complete lack of cooperation."

With that he swung from the laboratory and was gone.

Merva remained grimly silent for several moments after the laboratory door had closed, then she crossed over to the life energy machine and set to work to devise the electrical circuit to give it protection in case of emergency. This was a task that was destined to occupy her for some hours and in the meantime Exodus had gone in search of Vilnia. He found her in her accustomed place in the conning tower. He looked and felt rather irritated as he studied her innocent young face as she stared outwards towards the stars.

"Why do you have to spend so much time in here?" he demanded roughly. "Don't you realise that you are a scientist just like the rest of us and for that reason you should be constantly at my side helping me in the tasks which I have to perform. Instead of that I find you here looking out on to infinity. What do you expect to gain by doing that?"

Vilnia turned and looked at him wistfully.

"Have you never liked to be alone with your thoughts, Exodus?"

"What I like and what I get are two very different things, Vilnia. Usually I have so many things to work out I just haven't time to be alone with my thoughts. You seem to forget that I am one of the prime movers in this great scheme of vengeance against the Earth. I have no time to spend gazing out on to infinity."

"From which I assume you wish me to help you with something or other?"

"I had thought of that possibility," Exodus admitted, and then he hesitated. Finally he shook his head. "Upon reflection I'm afraid you would be more of a hindrance than help. I suppose it is a wife's purpose to help her husband but only within the limits which she understands and you couldn't possibly understand a cosmic energy generator."

Vilnia looked at him quickly. "And what in heaven's name do you want a thing like that for? Or is it all part of that plot you mentioned to be rid of your mother?"

"Plot I mentioned?" Exodus frowned a little, then he gave a sudden start. "Just a minute!"

Reaching forward he caught Vilnia's shoulders fiercely and forced her to look at him. "Tell me something, Vilnia. Did you by any chance tell mother that I had mentioned casually that I didn't forever intend to be under her domination?"

Vilnia was silent, looking away, until Exodus' rough hand forced her to once again look at him.

"Well?" he demanded, "I'm asking you a question. Don't sit there like a mute!"

"As a matter of fact I did," Vilnia replied, sighing. "Now that you do know the worst thing you can do is kill me and I don't suppose you will do that. At least, not until a child has been born!"

Exodus lowered his hands and pondered. "This," he said slowly, "explains a great deal. Mother was particularly cautious when I asked her if I could study the life energy machine. I just couldn't understand why then, but I do now. She must believe from what you have told her that I intend to do something to stop her receiving the energy, which she must have. As a matter of actual fact nothing could be further from my thoughts. The trouble is that I'm now going to be greatly delayed in the construction of my cosmic generator, thanks to your infernal interference. Why did you have to betray my confidence like that?" he demanded savagely.

"I have a respect for my conscience, Exodus, even if you have not. I just could not hear of a plot like that directed against my mother-in-law without warning her of what was coming."

"How very touching," Exodus sneered, "and also how very unconvincing. I can hardly imagine any person in whose fate you are less concerned than my mother's—unless it be mine."

Vilnia got to her feet and shrugged her shoulders.

"If you don't mind. Exodus, I'm finding this conversation extremely odious. I would prefer to talk to you when you are in a calmer mood."

"Don't you dare adopt that tone to me!" he barked, catching her arm and swinging her back to him. "You seem to have forgotten one fact—you're my wife now, and as such entirely under my dictation. That is the law of the ship and there is certainly going to be no exception in your case. I'll tell you why you betrayed me to my mother," he went on, tightening his hold so fiercely on Vilnia's arm that she gave a little gasp, "because you thought by doing that to curry favour with her. You thought she would grant you favours, my dear, didn't you?"

"I certainly thought it might make her hate me less," Vilnia retorted fiercely, "and let go of my arm, you're hurting me." She snatched it away savagely.

"Ah, so Vilnia has a little fire after all," Exodus sneered, dropping his hand. "I thought you had more intelligence than the others and therefore a little more spirit. It pleases me to see it, but it does *not* please me to know that you have started off our married life by repeating a merely casual remark in the way you have. Suppose we get one thing straight, Vilnia, here and now—do you to the end of your days prefer to be dominated by my mother or by me?"

"I may not be dominated by either," she answered, ambiguously.

Exodus grinned broadly. "Can it be that the little Vilnia is conceiving some way of disposing of me as well as my mother? You haven't the brains or the courage, my dear, so don't waste your time. You're just like the rest of your generation, spineless and lazy good-for-nothings. Haven't you noticed how they all react, why it is that I am the strongest of the generation? Why it is that you are all weak physically and the rest of your colleagues of the same generation as well? The reason is not far to seek.

"That extraction of energy from you and the others when you were children has had the inevitable reaction of producing feeble adult life. Not enough to incapacitate but enough to reduce that immense virility of purpose which one has come to expect of adult scientists in this day and age."

Vilnia smiled faintly to herself and Exodus gave an angry look.

"I was not aware that I had said anything funny!"

"No, Exodus, you didn't say anything funny. I was just thinking how odd it would be if our lack of virility makes it that no children are born. That would be a great tragedy for you and your mother, wouldn't it?"

Exodus started. "That must not happen at any price! It would ruin everything!"

"As far as I am concerned I could very easily ruin everything by leaping out of the airlock into the void. What would you do then, Exodus?"

He stared at her, unbelieving. It seemed impossible that so frail a girl with so gentle a voice could even conceive of flinging herself into the sub-zero of interstellar space.

"Don't worry," she said, gently, "I shan't do that. Not because I am afraid to do so but because—believe it or not—it would give me pleasure to have a child of my own in whom I could take an interest despite the fact that he or she will become nothing more or less than a tool of your mother and you. Nevertheless it would perhaps help to fill the aching void, the awful longing that is within me.... It will give me something to cherish and to love.

"To go through life as I am now, not caring for or being cared for by anybody is absolute hell. You can't see it from my point of view because you have power and this fantastic plan of vengeance. But the rest of the girls aboard this vessel feel like I do, and indeed some of the young men too. They're not all at one with this idea of vengeance, believe me: it seems to have become centred only between you and your mother now. There still remains with us the memory of that experiment in our childhood when quite unable to help ourselves we were sacrificed to the Moloch of your mother's thirst for revenge. And," Vilnia added simply, with an upward lift of her wide eyes, "the scheme will never work out, Exodus, you know."

"Never work out! Don't be ridiculous! The planning through the endless years, the absolute meticulous regard to detail, the vast scientific machines, the enormous expenditure of mental energy, the checking by electronic brains of every figure we shall ever make, and you say it I can never work out! Of all the fool things you've said, Vilnia, that is decidedly the most foolish."

Vilnia sat down again looking at the stars. "In any case it doesn't matter to me," she shrugged. "I shall not be alive when that time comes. But when the time does come you'll remember what I have said. It cannot work out...."

"Then suppose you tell me why not?"

"I don't know why not. If I did I'd tell you. I just happen to know, that's all. It's a sort of instinct."

"I never did believe in woman's intuition," Exodus retorted, bitterly. With that he swung away and left the conning tower hurrying out to the adjoining section of the laboratory which was devoted entirely to draughtsmanship and the drawing board stage of the various weapons of destruction intended for the ultimate vengeance.

Vilnia watched him go and smiled sadly to herself.

And the ship fled on....

* * * *

Weeks—months—years— In one respect Vilnia had proved incorrect. Children had been born, her own included, and as far as could be told by the medical machine aboard the vessel each one of them was entirely robust and physically perfect in every detail. Whatever the lack of vitality in the parents, occasioned by their losing so much vital energy in their youth, it had apparently not been handed on to the offspring.

Five years had gone since that speaking-of-minds in the conning tower and now Exodus and Vilnia had reached full maturity and twenty-three years of age. As far as Vilnia was concerned the difference was hardly apparent except that she had perhaps more development and was indeed about an inch taller than she had been.

It was in Exodus that the change was so obvious. Big as a youth he was immense as a man and almost an exact duplicate of the mighty Rigilus who had once ruled the world and the solar system. He was majestic, dominant and entirely cruel, a perfect combination of his mother and father. Where Rigilus had had the tolerance, Exodus had none and where Rigilus had carried most people along with him and benefited them thereby, Exodus had become a figure of terror, a prowler aboard the mighty space machine; his steely eyes always alert for the smallest fault and his authority absolutely unchallenged since he always had his mother to back him.

In the five years he had been more than busy particularly concerned with the designing of his cosmic energy generator, the final plan of which his mother had herself checked and found to be entirely accurate. Her approval of the plan had taken place some years before and immediately afterwards Exodus had set to work on the actual building of the equipment in the empty storage hold which he had selected as his site.

He had never allowed anyone to come and watch him during the construction of that apparatus but at times either his mother or Vilnia had accidently come upon him at work and had seen a heavily suited figure, complete with hood and gigantic gauntlets, busily at work like some ultra modem Faust as he tamed the inconceivable energies of outer space and bent them to his will within the enormous generator which he had devised.

Even yet the generator itself was not complete, nor for that matter were his experiments for cosmic radiation. To be entirely satisfied with the apparatus's power he had to find something living upon which to test it, and this was the problem at the moment that held him up.

He was in the midst of checking up the apparatus on one occasion when Vilnia came in to him—or rather paused in the doorway of the storage hold somewhat awe-stricken by the spectacular flashings of power rippling from the masses of coils from the great towers of insulators.

"Exodus," Vilrúa called, motioning, "your mother wants both of us at once!"

Since Exodus was not in his heavily insulated suit he heard her words clearly enough. He turned sharply.

"Is it imperative? I'm extremely busy at the moment."

"She seems to think it is. Yes, we'd better go!"

Before very long they had reached Merva's apartment and found her in the midst of checking a list of names.

"You sent for us, mother?" Exodus asked, briefly, making no attempt to hide the fact that he did not like interruption in his work.

"I had no particular need to do," Merva answered, calmly. "I just thought that you would like to know that within an hour I have decided to use your child, and of course the other children which have been born, for the purposes of energy extraction. I have not informed the others of my intention since I did not deem it altogether necessary. I have merely done so in your case as a matter of courtesy."

Neither Exodus nor Vilnia said anything. On Vilnia's face there was a resigned, wearied look, but Exodus' expression was entirely different. It was grimly resolute and his eyes had become unmistakably obstinate.

"Just as well you told us, mother. I have no intention of allowing our son, Orius, to become one of the energy suppliers."

Vilnia gave a surprised glance and Merva's face set hard.

"If this is a joke, Exodus, I fail completely to see the point of it."

"It's no joke, believe me."

"But you agreed long ago that your child should be used, along with the others—"

"I said that then because there was no immediate need of Orius, but now that it has come to the actual time I've changed my mind. You seem to forget that Orius is different from the other children in that he is the son of the ruler's son and therefore in a class by himself—just as I was in a class by myself when those of my generation were subjected to the energy extraction."

"Believe me," Vilnia put in, seeing the angry look in Merva's eyes, "this is as much a surprise to me as it is to you. Exodus has never mentioned to me that he had any objections to Orius being used as an energy producer so I...."

"Be quiet," Exodus commanded. "I'm in charge of this situation, Vilnia, not you."

"Orius is as much my son as he is yours," she reminded him.

"That is beside the point. The fact remains, mother, that that is my decision, so you will have to make do with the other three children."

"It's not a question of making do," Merva retorted. "We have just got to have all the children if we are to have enough energy to carry on. It takes four children per generation to keep the energy at a safe level for both you and myself."

Exodus shrugged. "I am still not making any change in my decision. Is there anything else about which you wished to see us?"

Merva did not respond; her stony expression was quite sufficient.

"Come, Vilnia," Exodus said, briefly, jerking his head to her and he ushered her out of the room in front of him. Once they were out in the corridor Vilnia looked at him questioningly.

"Defiance of your mother can have grave consequences, Exodus. Not only in the matter of the kind of reprisal that your mother might take but also because there will not be enough energy for you and her to maintain your almost eternal life. I cannot understand why you are so obstinate in the face of such an issue."

"I know perfectly well what I am doing," he answered coldly. "I would tell you a great deal more, Vilnia, but I am afraid I do not trust you. I haven't forgotten the incident when you informed my mother of a certain passing remark of mine. Obviously you can never be expected to share any secrets with me again after that.

"One thing I will tell you, however—I will not allow Orius to be subjected to this energy reduction because of the severe repercussions it has in later life. You yourself are a good example of it and most certainly the other couples are aboard this vessel. They are listless, not particularly strong physically, and their mental quota is far below what it ought to be. I do not intend to see Orius reduced to a state like that either for mother or anybody else. Our child has be supremely strong and powerful—"

"That surely is a small issue to weigh against the eternal life of your mother and yourself," Vilnia protested. "I just can't understand your viewpoint on this at all, Exodus."

"Then don't try, and leave us to handle the situation."

Vilnia was silent, her eyes downcast. Exodus gave her a brief, rather irritated glance.

"Where is Orius at the moment? You saw him last."

"He's in the main nursery along with the other children."

"Then get him immediately and lock him in our room. After that, return to the storage hold where I am building the generator. There is something I want you to do which will help me considerably."

Vilnia did not raise an objection, because the years of domination that she had suffered caused her to obey Exodus' command immediately and she hurried off down the corridor.

He watched her go, then his face as expressionless as though it were carved in teak he went on his way back to the storage hold where his cosmic generator was located. Here he busied himself for a while with the controls and switches, testing the immense surges of energy that passed through the apparatus. At length Vilnia came in hesitantly and paused just beyond the threshold, once again feeling that inner terror at the sight of the man-made chained lightning writhing between the positive and negative poles.

"Well?" Exodus glanced at her briefly. "Did you do as I asked?"

"Yes. I put him in our compartment and locked him in and here is the key." Vilnia held it up for a moment then dropped it in the pocket of her slacks. Exodus nodded in satisfaction, then a thought seemed to strike him.

"Come to think of it, Vilnia, I think I'll take that key myself and if you wish to know why it is still because, unfortunately, I cannot trust you. If mother were to summon you and make certain demands upon you, you would immediately concede—partly from fear, and partly from the hope that you might curry favour with her. I don't intend to allow that to happen. The key please...." He held out his hand with sudden emphasis.

Puzzled, and somehow not entirely able to believe his reason for wanting the key, Vilnia nevertheless obeyed and handed it over. He slipped it in his pocket and nodded in satisfaction.

"Now for the task with which I wanted you to help me." He switched off the terrifying display of the apparatus and Vilnia breathed more freely. As he jerked his head to her she came forward, pausing when she had at length reached the highly conductive grating between the positive and negative poles.

"You see that big bolt there?" Exodus asked, indicating an enormous octagonal bolt at floor level which was standing up partly from its socket—then as Vilnia nodded he crossed to the bench and picked up a heavy wrench, handing it across to her.

"I want you to tighten up that whilst I get underneath the foundation here and secure the nut on the other side. It has been giving me trouble from the very start and it takes two people to be able to do it properly. I don't think you're likely to be able to learn much about this apparatus from just a simple operation like this. Do you think you can manage it?"

"Oh yes, I think I can manage that," Vilnia agreed, taking no offence at the immense sarcasm in his voice, and so saying, she fixed the wrench on the bolt sides and made the necessary adjustments. Exodus watched her for a moment and then moved away. Vilnia was too intent on her task to notice what he was doing, otherwise she would have wondered why he crossed to the switchboard.

In the next few moments she had no chance to wonder about anything at all for with a relentless hand he closed the main knife switch and between the two poles there flashed a bewildering coruscation of lavender flame and crackling energy.

Vilnia had just time to give one vast scream and she realised she was completely trapped. The next moment there was a blinding flash and the powerful earthing apparatus absorbed the tremendous surge of current. Exodus blinked a little, his mouth a straight and determined line, his eyes fixed on the space between the opposite poles where Vilnia had been at work.

There was nothing there except the big wrench that she had dropped. Vilnia had completely disappeared. With a jerk Exodus pulled out the knife switch and just for a moment put a hand over his moist forehead.

"Sorry, Vilnia," he muttered, "but somebody had to try it someday! At least, you can be written down in cosmic history as the one who gave her life to prove that undiluted cosmic energy can indeed destroy flesh and blood completely. In fact," he continued, musing, "one might almost say that this is a case of two birds with one stone. I have made sure that Vilnia can never betray me again, and on the other hand I have proved the efficiency of this instrument."

The problem of explanations as to what had happened to Vilnia did not bother him in the least. He would make vague references to an accident just as his mother had once done many years before him when explaining away the death of Rigilus, and as far as he was concerned he felt no remorse.

Vilnia had served her purpose in that she had produced Orius, yet another cog in the great scheme of revenge and her weakness for giving away secrets was something that need no longer be feared. Yet despite the fact that he had so inhumanly proved the efficacy of his cosmic radiation apparatus, Exodus did not immediately rush to tell his mother the news.

For this he had a particularly good reason, and it was not because she would now be engaged in withdrawing energy from the various children. Actually there was no need for his mother to know about the cosmic radiation equipment for the simple reason that he did not intend her to live beyond a few hours more.

Here lay the explanation for him refusing to grant that energy should be drawn from Orius. He knew perfectly well that the energy drawn from the other children would not be sufficient to keep himself and his mother supplied indefinitely, but if only he himself were concerned there would be ample and it was in this direction that his plans lay. He made no immediate moves however, biding his time until he was certain that his mother has retired to rest. This meant that everybody else had also retired in accordance with pre-arranged schedule, and that the children from whom energy had been extracted were now in the main nursery, recovering from the effects thereof. This meant that he had the vessel entirely to himself and so he went to work deliberately and with the actions of a man who had long had this plan in mind.

Going to the main storage hold he brought forth a spacesuit and rapidly clambered into it, twisting the transparent helmet into place and afterwards checking the air supply apparatus to make sure it was in perfect condition.

From the wall rack he took down a powerful radiant energy cutter that was actually a super modem modification of the old time oxy-acetylene welder. The apparatus was capable of generating an intolerable heat searching enough to cut through the armoured hull of the space machine's exterior plates. Armed in this wise Exodus silently made his way to the emergency exit of the machine and eventually was successful in impelling himself to the exterior of the vessel.

Once here the slight gravitation of the vessel drew down on his enormous metal boots so that he was clamped to the outer plates like a fly on the ceiling. This was not the first time that he had ventured to the outside, so the experience lacked the wonder of the first occasion. Nevertheless there was even yet an immense fascination in thus standing as a lone figure in the void, surrounded by the endless hosts of stars.

However, the last thing on his mind was to admire the view. He took merely a cursory glance about him and then walked deliberately forward remaining upright no matter which angle he chose to take on the vessel because of the constant pull of gravity on his feet. In this manner he walked along the side of the machine until he eventually came to the deeply sunken round porthole which he knew was the one window belonging to his mother's bedroom.

Descending to his knees he peered through the thick glass and after a while could descry the sleeping form of his mother vaguely visible in the safety light which was left glowing in every part of the vessel, at all times. Her back was towards him, which was an advantage and the bedclothes were pulled up roughly towards her shoulders.

"I have been a long time getting round to this, mother," he murmured, unhooking the radiant energy gun from his belt, "but now, necessity compels me to act."

The actual execution of his plan was only the work of a moment when all he did was to direct the blast of the radiant energy gun straight at the thick glass of the porthole. Instantly it splintered, but not inwards. The javelins of shattered glass, each of them nearly an inch thick, were blasted outwards by the atmospheric pressure within the cabin itself, and thereafter shimmered in space like floating shards of silver paper.

The effect was extraordinary and fairy-like and rendered even more fantastic by the fact that the pieces thereafter drifted slowly back until they were adhering to the side of the ship, drawn as usual by the eternal law of mass.

Peering through the now entirely uncovered porthole. Exodus could still faintly see his mother lying motionless on the bed. Evidently the end had come to her without her making so much as a movement. The sudden evaporation of the air from the compartment and the inrush of the interstellar void must have made death instantaneous—and, filled with the sober knowledge of this fact, Exodus made his way back into the vessel and then continued along the corridor until he had come to his mother's compartment.

Working with great caution and still dad in his spacesuit he pulled down the emergency switch which caused airtight metal slides to drop into place on both sides of him in the corridor, thereby sealing off the rest of the ship from the outrush of air from this little square of corridor when he opened the door of his mother's compartment.

This was only the work of a moment and he crept forward into the star shine in the air denuded space, looking about him upon the tumbled ornaments, shifted furniture, and tangled bedclothes, all of which had been dragged in the direction of the shattered porthole by the abrupt out-rush of the air under its normal pressure of 14 pounds to the square inch.

Switching on his torch he moved forward with the beam directed on the still figure in the bed, and the nearer he moved the more puzzled he became. There was something odd about it, something unnaturally stiff. In a matter of seconds he realised the truth.

It was nothing more than a dummy, and yet the thing was so lifelike that he found it next to impossible to realise that it was one. He reached out his gauntletted hand and touched it and that satisfied him. It was a brilliant creation in wax, an exact replica of his mother, so wonderfully done that it might have made the one-time famous Madame Tussaud extremely envious.

But why? How?

Exodus straightened up, breathing hard, trying to imagine how his mother could possibly have known of the plan that he had had in mind. He had never hinted at it to anybody; and Vilnia had certainly not had the chance to give anything away. So how then had it happened that the tables had been turned upon him? And where was his mother now?

It was as he tried to wrestle with this problem that the radio equipment within his space suit suddenly picked up the sound of his mother's voice.

"Not quite so clever as you thought, Exodus, are you? For your information I have you under full observation, your image being picked up by infra red rays and re-radiated to me. At the present moment I am in one of the small emergency holds of the ship that, unknown to you, has been a comfortable bedroom for me for many years past. Indeed ever since the day when Vilnia warned me that you had designs upon my life. Not only have I taken precautions to guard the life energy machine, but I have also taken care to guard my own life as well by this very simple strategy.

"You have never known about this second bedroom of mine, which is reached by the simple process of my descending through the door of a trap in my normal bedroom and so into the lower regions of the vessel and my private bedroom compartment. In here I have all the necessary instruments with which to study the entire ship and with which to keep a constant eye on the activities of those around me. It is a sad reflection on the lack of trust in me that I have had to resort to such measures.

"The dummy which you observe in the bed has an electrical contact so that the impact of the beam of your torch, and later on when you touched the dummy itself, started up an electrical circuit and awakened me, warning me that you were prowling about in my bedroom—my normal bedroom that is. I had only to switch on the infra red television and I am now looking at you, your spacesuited figure clearly illumined by the infra red rays which you of course cannot see. My voice is reaching you by normal radio waves and of course they are reacting upon the radio equipment in your suit. Now, Exodus, what have you to say for yourself? I observe from the state of my room that you have shattered the glass of the porthole. I gather that it was your delightful intention to destroy me by suffocation and interstellar vacuum...."

Exodus listened to all this in a kind of frozen wonderment, still not fully able to believe that he had been completely tricked. This was not the matter that worried him as the fear of the kind of reprisal his mother would take. He had exposed his hand completely and now she would be in complete control of the situation.

"You see, Exodus," came her dry voice, "I am much more indispensable than you would imagine. However, you are my son, and despite this villainous attack upon me, by which I imagine you hoped you would gain full power, I am not yet prepared to say what kind of action should be taken about you. I think it better that we should discuss that in a proper manner. Slide the emergency shield over the porthole, switch the air pressure tanks on to normal, remove the slide from the corridor, which I presume is in position—and join me in the lounge in five minutes."

With that the radio communication ceased with an abrupt click. Exodus compressed his lips, muttered something to himself, then moved across to the porthole to put the first of his orders into execution.

Within the stipulated time he had done everything as instructed and. with the air pressure once again normal he rid himself of his spacesuit and on the way to the lounge looked once in the compartment where Orius was sleeping. Apparently the child was quite undisturbed, so evidently Merva had not attempted to use him for the energy-extraction.

Silently withdrawing again, but not troubling this time to lock the door, Exodus went on his way to join his mother in the lounge.

CHAPTER SIX

COSMIC COLLISION

"I suppose," Merva said, her face grim, "that at this moment you are considering it a matter of profound regret that I did not die as you intended? In trying to be rid of me, Exodus, you have a great deal more on your hands than you imagine."

"I should have known that," he said, quietly, for once genuinely contrite. "On the other hand I do not make any apology for having tried to dispose of you. Neither of us likes sharing power and I think were the circumstances reversed you would unhesitatingly have endeavoured to do the same thing."

"Probably," Merva admitted, shrugging. And as on that other long gone occasion their eyes met each other steadily—and again as before, neither showed the least sign of flinching.

"So now," Merva said, "we face an impasse. Just before I retired I made it my business to check up on the amount of energy gained from those children upon whom I experimented. I regret to say that the gain is so slight that there is still only enough energy left for one of us to complete the thousand year voyage and make the journey back home to exact revenge."

Exodus looked puzzled. "But how does that come about? I understood you to say that there would be a great increase in the amount of energy once you had—"

"Yes, and that was exactly what I believed. Unfortunately, however, these children are by no means as virile and strong as were the preceding generation from which you came. They are the children of parents who have been greatly reduced in vitality due to the energy extraction in their youth, and as far as I can see this kind of defect will become progressive in that the children of each generation of children will become weaker due entirely to this exchange. Nor is it something that can be altered by skipping one generation in between and thereby giving one batch of children the chance to catch up on lost energy Indeed, Exodus, as far as I can see there is only one chance left...."

"And that is?"

"Give the children a few more years to develop and mature and then again take energy from them. Even the inclusion of Orius, which you are against, would make little difference to the full quota, so he can be discounted. It will be a tremendous risk since they may die as the result of a double energy extraction in the course of their young lives—but it is something that has to be chanced. Their parents must also be informed immediately that more children are required as fast as possible, who can stand by in the event of these present children failing to supply a second extraction."

"In fact, taking it all round," Exodus said, drily, "it would probably have solved a great many problems if I had succeeded in my efforts to eliminate you."

"Probably, only you did not. The best thing we can do is examine these children, see how they are recovering from the extraction, and then make the necessary arrangements to restore them to full health and vigour as rapidly as possible."

Exodus nodded. At the moment there was nothing else he could do but fall in entirely with his mother's plans. For the time being his own schemes had gone completely awry and he was more or less forced to obey her until there dawned on him some fresh line of action.

Turning, he followed his mother from the lounge and then down the long passage to the compartment that had been turned into a small dormitory where the children had been left to recover. When Merva switched on the light it appeared that they were still sleeping and with unusual heaviness. In a few seconds Merva had discovered the truth and turned startled eyes to Exodus as he stood immediately behind her.

"These children are dead," she said slowly, straightening up and for a moment or two she stared in front of her as though she could not believe it. "And from the coldness of them they have been dead for some hours. I suppose that this couldn't be some trickery of yours?" she demanded.

"Not this time," Exodus answered, coldly. "I have not concerned myself in the least with the children: I was too busy trying to dispose of you."

"This puts us in a disastrous situation," Merva muttered. "Only enough energy for one of us, and even if more children were born by the present parents there is no guarantee that they will be any more virile than these who have died from reaction. What bit of energy that they may be able to give off will not add much to the store that we have at the moment. And yet more children are an absolute necessity otherwise there will be none to grow to maturity to produce more children. The whole thing is nothing more or less than a vicious circle."

"As far as I can see," Exodus commented, after a long, thoughtful silence, "there is only one way out of this one mother, now that these children are dead. Either you or I have to finish the journey and exact the vengeance upon which we are both set. You are quite convinced that there is enough energy for *one*?"

"Yes," Merva admitted, tonelessly. "One will be able to manage very easily."

"Very well then, which of us is to die?"

There was a heavy silence in the chamber and Merva did not immediately respond. She stood looking down at the silent children then she wandered slowly out into the corridor again with Exodus coming up behind her. He closed the door of the compartment with a sudden air of resolution.

"This is not a matter which can be escaped," he said bluntly. "We have to decide this issue once and for all."

"And what do you suggest?" Merva asked bitterly.

"That we draw lots, or something like that?"

"We might do worse."

Merva moved uncertainly, plainly quite unable to make up her mind. Exodus watched her narrowly. He was quite determined that no matter which way the issue went—that even if he were the one to whom it should fall to eliminate himself—he would not do so. He believed, that rightly or wrongly, as the younger of the two, it should be Merva's task to give way.

Then suddenly as they both strove to find a way round the difficulty there came a sound in the empty, silent reaches of the great space liner.

It began as a distant buzzing which rapidly travelled the length of the ship and changed to a strident ringing noise coming from a dozen or more alarm bells scattered in various parts of the vessel.

Just for a moment Merva and Exodus looked at one another, since it was the first time that the alarm bell had sounded during the colossal journey from Earth. It meant that somewhere outside the ship there was danger approaching either in the shape of a meteor or in the form of some cosmic hulk or other.

"Quick," Merva said abruptly, all else forgotten for the moment, "the control room! We've got to find out what this means!"

She and Exodus fled down the remaining stretch of corridor just as in other parts of the ship other members of the party stirred lazily and wondered what all the commotion was about. Not that they troubled themselves to find out; for one thing they were too lazy minded and physically weary, and for another they were content to leave any threat to their safety to the handling of Merva and Exodus—so they made no move. But as the alarm bells ceased ringing, on Merva disconnecting the circuit they went to sleep again, not in the least concerned. As yet they had no idea their children had died.

In the control room, however, there was very real concern since both Merva and Exodus knew what damage might be done to the ship if it were struck by a wandering hulk.

Merva immediately set the radar scarching-equipment into action, which was in itself linked to the alarm system in that it sent out an 'echo' beam for a million miles ahead of the vessel and it reflected back to the ship the presence of any object which might be in its path.

Immediately the apparatus was switched on there appeared on the reflective screen a shimmering point of light, which was gradually expanding with the seconds. Instantly Exodus slipped the measuring scale into operation and then gave a whistle of alarm.

"Right in our track!" he gasped. "And from the look of it it's a large asteroid nearly a thousand miles in diameter! Since we cannot by any conceivable method turn the vessel aside—the controls being locked to the electronic brain—we'll have to switch on the repeller shields and hope for the best. Personally, the velocity we're going at and with that thing dead centred in our tracks I don't think there is much we can do!"

He crossed swiftly to the master switchboard and thrust into contact the switch controlling the repeller field. This meant that the vessel was immediately encased in a cocoon of energy outside, which should prove effective enough to deflect the approaching obstacle—or more correctly deflect the ship itself from the *course* of the obstacle. An object as big as that was most likely to be unmoved, rather the recoil would tend to shift the vessel itself from its predetermined course. After which the electronic brain would make the necessary corrections for having swerved off the charted path and would eventually restore the machine to its normal position in space.

"That thing," Merva said, looking at the screen, "is heading towards us at thousands of miles a second, partly on account of its own velocity and partly on account of our speed. In about five minutes we'll know the worst. We might as well put our space suits on in case the air pressure should happen to escape."

Exodus dived across to the storage cupboard, afterwards dragging out a couple of the suits and handing one to his mother. Both of them quickly bundled themselves into the voluminous folds and screwed on the helmets, by which time the distended glow on the radar echo screens showed that the object was almost upon them.

"We'd show a great deal more sense if we got out of this control room," came Merva's voice through the audio-phone. "That thing is advancing straight towards us and the control room will be the first place to get hit."

Exodus nodded promptly and headed out of the doorway and along the corridor. He expected that his mother was immediately behind him, but she delayed for a second or two to check on the fact that the repeller circuit was working at full voltage. And it was in those few seconds that the thing happened.

Abruptly, as he was nearing the end of the corridor, his goal being the storage hold in which was standing the immense cosmic radiation generator, Exodus found himself flung from his feet by a monstrous concussion. The impact of it hurled him against the wall and dropped him half senseless to the floor.

As he lay there struggling to recover his wits he noticed the lights bobbing in and out, due entirely to the immense electrical reaction from the power plant as the repeller shields strove to fling aside the cause of the immense disturbance. These were occurrences which happened in a matter of seconds and then he suddenly found himself being lifted to his feet and dragged along the corridor as though by an invisible rope. Immediately he went to work to check his slithering advance as he realised the cause of the trouble.

In the control room a great rent had evidently been torn in the ship and the air was escaping through it, pulling everything movable along with it. With a tremendous effort Exodus managed to scramble to the wall and thereafter to brace himself to prevent his being sucked through the gap that must exist in the control room. By the time he had been dragged this far, however, the air from the corridor and the control room had completely escaped and the danger for him was over.

Grateful for the spacesuit that had saved him from asphyxiation, he tumbled into the control room and looked about him—almost immediately gazing upon a scene of total chaos and ruin.

In the side of the vessel a great ragged hole lay open to the stars. The meteor or cosmic hulk or whatever it had been, had now passed on its way leaving behind it the most appalling damage.

Nor was the material damage the main thing, for Merva lay face down on the floor, jammed against a fixed stool by way of her legs being either side of it. There was a rip down the back of her space suit where a jagged metal chunk from the roof had sliced through it with its razor keen edge. Instantly Exodus hurried forward, dropping on his knees and gathering the limp form of his mother in his arms. Not that there was any point in doing this for with the abrupt evaporation of air from her suit and the inrush of interstellar vacuum her lungs had ceased to function.

She lay with her eyes closed behind the transparent helmet, her face marble white in the tautness of death! Still unsatisfied Exodus slipped a detector from under one of the hooks on his belt and thrusting it inside his mother's suit held it against her heart. The delicate needle that normally responded distinctly to the lowest of heartbeats remained at zero. There was no question of it any more—his mother was dead.

Dazed, and not quite sure whether this was good fortune or not as far as his mother was concerned, he finally got to his feet again and surveyed the wreckage about him Apparently the main electronic brain switchboard connected to the controls had escaped damage, but most of the smaller instruments, such as the radar detector and the radio equipment, were shattered to fragments and also several of the upright stanchions supporting the roof had buckled like tapers before a hot fire.

Stumbling about amidst the wreckage, Exodus finally reached the doorway again and so made his way out into the corridor, his intention being to inform the others aboard the vessel of what had happened. To his amazement, as he advanced down the corridor, he beheld the other men and women in the corridor itself, sprawled about the floor in various positions, the doors of their different apartments swinging open. Immediately it dawned upon him what had happened. The concussion of the ship had aroused each one of them, as it could hardly have failed to do, and they had quickly left their compartments to discover the cause of the trouble, not knowing that the air had been sucked from the main body of the ship.

They had instantly stumbled into the interstellar airlessness and collapsed, dying in just same fashion as Merva had done. And amongst them was the small form of Orius! Exodus looked down at him, stunned. The child too, then, had emerged from his unlocked compartment to investigate the commotion, and now....

Exodus compressed his lips, struggling hard to comprehend the fact that, next to himself, he had lost the one life he valued most. Exodus himself had heard nothing of all this for in the insulation of his spacesuit he had been unable to pick up any sound—and for that matter no sound could have reached him anyway since there existed a complete vacuum—all the air, save for the little remaining in the few bedrooms, having by now been sucked out into the inexorable vacuum of outer space.

Indeed, things had happened so fast that Exodus hardly knew what to do next. It was only by degrees that it dawned upon him that he was the only living being aboard the vessel. And, individual person though he was, the thought of it gave him just a little fear for the moment, as the immense aloneness slowly filtered into his mind.

He was the one living being in the uncharted depths of infinity, and as such, the only living person who could ever bring the great scheme of vengeance to a successful conclusion. Somehow the idea of vengeance seemed infinitely far away at the moment. His immediate predicament was the one thing that demanded consideration.

Finally, after careful consideration of the situation, Exodus made his first moves. To begin with there were the various bodies to dispose of and these presented no problem since he had only to take them to the ejection chamber and so project them into the depths of space. After this he was indeed alone and he spent a couple of hours carefully examining the battered ship from end to end and determining which parts remained intact.

Altogether the damage was not so severe as he had at first suspected. The main source of trouble seemed to be in the control room, but otherwise most of the vital instruments, and particularly the machine tool equipment, were more or less in perfect condition. So, also, to his intense relief, was the life-energy equipment. The biggest trouble was the great rent torn in the mass of the vessel and before the ship could be considered void-worthy again that gap had got to be repaired—which of course it could easily be since the machine tool equipment was undamaged.

Of necessity he was still compelled to work in his spacesuit, which, mainly owing to the clumsiness of his gloves, slowed him up considerably in his efforts. Nevertheless he set about his task with a vigorous determination and at the end of eight hours continuous work he had completely rewelded a new section of plating across the gap and thoroughly tested it to prove that it was airtight. This done, he was able at last to turn on the air pressure tanks and finally as the gauges showed the normal 14 pounds to the square inch, he was able to clamber from the stuffy enveloping folds of his spacesuit.

His next concern was to obey the demands of Nature and have a meal and then a rest. For a moment or two when he finally awoke he found it almost impossible to realise that there was nobody else aboard the vessel. Never again, perhaps, throughout the whole of his more or less eternal life, would he be able to speak to anybody nor would anybody speak to him. A more absolute solitary confinement could hardly be imagined nor one more ironical.

Around him and the space machine loomed all the incredible endless vastness of infinity, yet he was one person alone with not a soul to speak to, with nothing to keep him company except his own thoughts. It was a situation which, but for the ceaselessly burning fire of revenge, might easily have driven him insane by its stark, staring loneliness. As it was, he was not disturbed, as yet. He was a man dedicated to a purpose and because of that purpose the frozen hand of loneliness did not descend too heavily upon him.

He prepared a meal for himself, ate it, and then considered his next moves. Finally he decided upon the entirely ordinary task of repairing the final damage in the control room—the reconstruction of the broken stanchions and the replacement, where possible, of the smaller shattered instruments.

Though these tasks were not immense in themselves they occupied him for several days of time and when they were done he was back again to his starting point: what must he do next?

Revenge—that was the issue. He had no idea how far his mother's plans had progressed but in the main he had left all preparations of that vengeance entirely to her. With her departed it was now his task to devise some formula of his own to wreak the most deadly retaliation possible upon the descendants of the Earthlings who had brought about this position. He found himself blaming the people of Earth for the fact that he was now alone, not into the least taking into account that cosmic disaster and nothing else was responsible for the fact that he alone was left out of all those who had been aboard the spaceship. Everything he thought of, everything he did, was incessantly concentrated upon that one relentless objective— vengeance.

"And I still maintain," he muttered, as he stood alone by the control room porthole looking out on to the void, "that the most satisfactory way of ensuring that that vengeance is complete in every detail is to have the cosmic generator made to produce the absolute maximum of cosmic radiation. At the moment, as I designed it, there can be enough power to destroy half the world in one blow. I shall go further.... I shall go on developing that apparatus through the years until I am satisfied that it can encompass the whole eight thousand mile diameter of Earth simultaneously. In that way two onslaughts from the cosmic projector will be sufficient to reduce every living being upon the planet to ashes. One blow upon the western hemisphere of the world and one blow on the Eastern hemisphere and nothing can survive. That, then, shall be my ideal—a generator which can encompass the world."

He mused over this for quite a while, smiling harshly to himself and then he turned his mind to other things. There was the second problem—how to get access to the life energy machine, and to restore it to working order.

It was this thought which got him on the move again from the control room until he came to the compartment which had constituted his mother's secret bedroom.

In here, even as she had said, were the various radio and television instruments by which she had been able to view every part of the ship, usually through the adoption of infrared radiation. He also quickly located the controls for the electrical barrier his mother had placed around the life-energy machine when not using it herself. Smiling grimly, he switched it off, then crossed to the metal cabinet against the wall and quickly set to work to destroy the strong lock by which it was fastened. Within it he found many stacks of papers, some of them making a certain amount of sense and others entirely incomprehensible since they were a jumble of mathematical equations. In the main they constituted designs and sketches for death-dealing weapons, some of which had already appeared in the laboratory to his knowledge and others that had apparently been abandoned through inability to finish them completely.

He also discovered that which he really sought—the vital crystalline bars, which needed to be restored to the life energy machine to make it operative.

Two vitally important matters then were ahead of him—the building up of his cosmic energy projector to double its output and the devising of a velocity formula for the return to Earth in a much quicker time. When he was not dealing with the one he could deal with the other, for they would be counter-balanced by the one being a manual job and the other mental, and thereby he could keep himself constantly occupied.

In this way, he told himself that all would be well and that he was absolutely self-sufficient and needed no company whatever. The very fact that he had to admit this to himself was, in a sense, a proof that loneliness was to a certain extent the one thing of which he was afraid.

Before he did anything definite he injected into himself a given quota of life-energy and, thus refreshed, he set to work with his cosmic ray generator. To double the amount of its power was something that he found upon analysis to be impossible. So, with dogged determination he set to work to build a second generator, an exact replica of the first one, and just as it had taken him many years to build the first one, so this second one occupied him for an almost similar length of time. He spent most of his working hours at it, only desisting when he found himself making mistakes. It was at these times that he abandoned the manual side of his activities and returned to the control room, there to concentrate upon the problem of returning to Earth.

He indeed faced a profound mental complexity because of the physical fact that 186,000 miles per second was the absolute velocity beyond which no object in the universe, including his space machine, could travel.

At the moment, although it was travelling at stupendous speed, it was only a mere fraction of the speed of light, and so it was going to take a thousand years to reach Alpha Centauri travelling at that constant velocity. Therefore, logically, it must demand a continuous *acceleration* until the speed of light was approached. Only then could the engine be switched off, and then he could coast at his optimum speed, almost the speed of light. A year at this speed, and he would cover almost a light year of distance, and since Alpha Centauri was just over four light years from Earth, it was clearly possible to get back to Earth within a reasonable time. The problem was in the time it would take to build up to that ultimate speed. Even though the ship was fitted with artificial gravity and acceleration nullifiers, they were not completely effective at higher accelerations. If he were not to kill himself under the strain of too great a constant acceleration, his rate of acceleration would have to be carefully calculated. And exactly the same factors would have to be taken into account in the matter of deceleration, otherwise he might overshoot the Earth solar system, and continue plunging through space.

At a rough estimate, the return trip would take the best part of another thirty years, but on board the ship—such were the vagaries of Relativity—that to Exodus, much less time would appear to pass.

Even at that some one thousand and thirty years would have passed since the departure from Earth. Civilisations would have undergone vast and almost unimaginable changes. Just the same he did not fear that any of the civilisations would have devised weapons so diabolically scientific that they would be able to counteract the stupendous blast of cosmic radiation that he had planned.

Accordingly, the only thing for him to do was to carry the problem as far as he could with his own equations and then feed them to the electronic brains, which were in the laboratory solely for the purpose of dealing with such profoundly complicated problems.

So, by this division of mental and manual energy, he managed somehow to strike an even balance. He was so constantly absorbed with either one or the other that the lack of company never troubled him. He even began to sense a certain god-like condition in his floating thus alone in the void, the ship now back on its original course and still hurtling with inconceivable velocity towards Alpha Centauri.

Even yet, despite the years that had passed, the binary star appeared no larger so stupendously far away was it in the cosmos. There was indeed something fantastic in this lone man consumed entirely with a longing for revenge. His desire for revenge was even more remarkable in that he had not been the direct recipient of the injustice of Earth people.

He was only the child of the recipient, but so thoroughly had Merva instilled her own invective into him, he was as profoundly resolved as she had been to bring the plan to a successful conclusion. The thought of perhaps returning to Earth and establishing communication, and perhaps even seeking a pardon and a possible return to the people of his mother world, never even occurred to him, even though it would certainly have been the sanest course. For by the time he finally arrived back on Earth it was quite possible that the original banishment into the void would have been completely forgotten. It would purely be a matter of interest to historians and certainly not to the then existent society of Earth. However, Exodus had made his decision, a decision that had been nurtured since boyhood and he refused to allow anything to divert him.

Ever and again as the months fled by he would take a long observation of the void through the rear windows of the machine, there to behold the bloated ashen corpses of those who had been ejected from the ship in the course of its journey. Rigilus, Vilnia, Drando, Hazalet, they were all there together with the various children, moving at the same velocity as the ship itself separated from it by only a few feet, chained eternally by its gravitation.

The sight of them made Exodus pause and wonder. Were they happier now than they had been? Were they still possessed of bodies somewhere in this enormous infinity: had they been recreated perhaps in fleshly form upon some far distant world? Had they still the thoughts of vengeance in their minds as he had?

These were the thoughts of a man alone in space and they were thoughts that lacked a certain coherence. With only himself to think about and with only revenge as his motivating power Exodus was slowly and relentlessly changing into a very strange being indeed.

And the ship sped on....

CHAPTER SEVEN

JOURNEY'S END

IN the course of another five years Exodus had his second cosmic generator half completed. Throughout that five years he had loomed amid the cascading cosmic energies like some creation from Dante's *Inferno*, clothed in his huge insulated and protective suit with the immense gauntlets and cowl-like helmet. At other times he had not been so cautious, particularly when the manipulation of some delicate and sensitive parts of the apparatus had demanded that his hands be absolutely unencumbered. Whether or not the cosmic radiation in which he had been exposed during these periods had done him any harm he did not know. Certainly he felt no worse physically, so he assumed that all was well.

During these five years he had also made tests of his bodily energy and had found that the life energy absorption that he gave himself at regular intervals were apparently keeping him at a more or less constant level. There was little if any breakdown of cellular material that would have proclaimed advancing age. He was, as near as he could tell, living at a permanent twenty three to twenty four years of age.

There was indeed only one thing which troubled him, and this only slightly, and that was sudden but very infrequent lapses of memory. He noticed it most when working with the cosmic ray generator, for on examining his notes he found several mathematical postulations which he had set down which he could not properly remember when he came to study them again.

To him it was a mystery, but he put it down to one of those quirks of mental computation that do happen even to the healthiest and most balanced of people.

It was also after the expiration of this five years that he discovered the electronic computers had at last produced an answer for the journey back to Earth, basing their conclusions upon the original figures that he had fed into them. In order to keep the accelerative strain to a tolerable level, it would take some fifteen years before the speed of light could be reached, and the engines switched off. Thereafter the vessel would coast a constant velocity for another three years, followed by an equal fifteen-year period of deceleration.

Added to this finding was given the profoundly complicated formula by which the atomic generator would have to be stepped up in stages to create the necessary power imperative for such a sustained acceleration. They also showed again in equations how it would be possible to change the general design of the atomic power plant to make it capable of dealing with this stupendous load.

To all these details Exodus gave profound attention, knowing as he did that there was more than enough fuel to make the journey, as very little had been used on the outward voyage.

So then he had another task added to the one upon which he was already engaged and both of them now were manual and therefore made no demands whatever upon his mental capacities.

Yet again then, he plunged into the maw of years dividing his time between the final construction of the second cosmic generator and making the necessary modifications to the power plant. And ever and again he still experienced those odd moments when he forgot a vital point and for the life of him could not remember it.

Naturally he wondered about it but he made no particular effort to solve it. Altogether it took him yet another five years to completely reconstruct the power plant and finish his cosmic ray generator. The matter of the power plant occasioned no difficulty since it was not operating, nor had it done so since the departure from Earth, except for the brief period of course correction following the cosmic collision. The vessel still maintained the velocity that it had reached at the highest point of acceleration when the power plant itself had automatically cut out. The dismantling of it had nothing to do with the electronic brain controlling the switchboard and therefore it had been possible for him to strip it right down and rebuild it to the pattern prescribed by the infallible computer.

But now these tasks were done, and through the advance porthole Alpha Centauri and its now faintly visible Proxima Centauri were slightly larger, which proved that the awful abyss of space was indeed being covered slowly and inevitably.

Even so there were hundreds of years that must go by before the goal would be reached and the switchboard would be unlocked from the mathematical monster that controlled it. More than once Exodus had played around with the idea of taking the risk of trying to dismantle that radio switchboard but always he had remembered his mother's warning, the warning which had been given to her by the original People's Prosecutor of Earth.

He had said that the removal of one part of the electronic brain on the switchboard would mean that that part would never be replaced and that the vessel would become entirely uncontrollable, finally crashing upon the nearest gravitational object. It was probably the truth and it certainly served as a powerful deterrent as far as Exodus was concerned.

In the end he decided against any dismantling. He would let the switchboard run its course. How then to bridge the hundreds of years which loomed before him and in which there was nothing particular for him to do, everything having been accomplished?

He had the cosmic ray generators ready for action when the time came, which he was convinced would be thoroughly efficacious, and he also had the means of returning to Earth infinitely faster than he had left it.

There was only himself to consider now and in its way this was probably one of the biggest problems of all. If he did not find a quick way to bridge the terrible gap between this point of space and the end of the journey he felt that his mind might become so overwhelmed with the vastness of the void that he might become unbalanced and so lose everything that he had so relentlessly and assiduously built up.

When the answer to this problem came to him it made him smile ironically. The solution presented itself when he was engaged in one of those rare observations to the rear of the ship by which means he viewed the space-ridden corpses of those who had long since been ejected.

Except for their bloated appearance, which had happened at the moment that air had been expelled from their bodies, they were as preserved as waxen figures by the vacuum of the interstellar void.

The corpses could be thus preserved without any signs of decomposition, so surely could a living being?

And from this sprang Exodus' conception of a deep freeze system by which he ought to be able to refrigerate himself and yet return to life hundreds of years later. Such methods had been used in the anaesthetic field on Earth, or so his mother had told him, so there seemed no reason why he could not develop that process himself. Further, and it was this which made him smile so ironically, it would mean that if he existed at such a low level he would be expending hardly any energy whatever.

Certainly not enough to need any of the life energy that was still stored in the apparatus. Had his mother been alive now, and had both of them put themselves in a deep freeze, the energy would have lasted out for both of them— However, that was in the past and it was the future that he had to deal with.

So immediately he set about the task of devising a deep freeze system and from it, once again helped by the electronic brains, he worked out how to convert one of the many spare chambers in the space machine into a suspended animation compartment. The system was reasonably simple and more or less automatic in that reliable thermostatic controls would gradually expel almost all the air from the compartment and allow the deadly vacuum of the void to seep in. For this purpose a special apparatus was required which after two years of experiment he finally managed to perfect. It meant that when the room was completely sealed he would gradually sink into a subzero state—a deep sleep on the edge of death itself. The final point was the linking to the electronic brain which governed the control board of an extension, so arranged that it would cause the thermostatic controls within the deep freeze chamber to cease their activity when the space machine was at last within range of Alpha Centauri.

This was a matter again calling for a considerable amount of concentration and over a year of work, but finally Exodus mastered it and was reasonably sure that once he placed himself within the deep sleep he would be aroused within a few hours of the electronic brain releasing its hold upon the control switchboard. By this manner, then, he could skip the hundreds of years that still intervened before the end of the journey and still be sure of awakening in time.

With methodical calm he went to work to make his final arrangements, locking everything up in all directions, though for what reason he did not really know, unless it was that he was taking precautions against the possibility of the ship again colliding with something, which would mean that if the various articles were locked up they would not be scattered in all directions.

Whether or not he himself would be awakened if such an alarm arose he did not know: that was the unknown risk he had to take. Perhaps in putting himself to sleep he might also be putting himself to death—he just had to accept this as one of the unpredictable elements.

So finally he settled down on the airbed and switched on the thermostatic controls, afterwards composing himself for the gradual descent into the deep sleep that would inevitably follow. Everything worked exactly as he had planned it would, and there was no painful sensation in his gradual descent into drowsiness, and finally sleep.

Indeed it was no more unusual in its development than the normal transition from the waking to the sleeping world. It seemed to him distinctly strange that at one moment he could feel himself sliding into unconsciousness and the next he seemed to be awakening again.

In between there appeared to be no gap, no consciousness of dreaming. No sensation, no anything. It even made him wonder if the apparatus had failed in any way and if he had come back to consciousness. Then when he glanced up at the subsidiary time clock on the wall and saw that the liquid crystal display showed that the thousand-year deadline had been reached, he knew that he had indeed slept over the hundreds of years and that this was the awakening as he had planned it

The moment had arrived evidently when the electronic brain was at last going to release the switchboard and make the vessel governable.

Exodus struggled up from the bed and by degrees managed to get enough strength together to open the clamped door and stumble outside into the long passageway. Still extremely dazed, and remarking to himself on the incredible amount of dust that had collected upon everything in the interval, he made his way into the control room. There, before doing anything else, he gave himself a good meal and then gazed at himself in the mirror upon the magnificent wealth of beard he had grown in the interval.

Since his energy expenditure had been so low his beard was not commensurate with having slept for hundreds of years, but nevertheless it was a magnificent crop. In the space of ten minutes, he had entirely rid himself of it and freshened up. Mentally alert, he turned to the switchboard and studied it.

Upon the top of the electronic brain control a red lamp was now glowing, showing that its influence was beginning to wane. Exodus pondered it for a while and then turned to the main porthole giving a start as he beheld the now quite near Alpha Centauri.

It loomed as a titanic blinding star whilst close beside it was the smaller Proxima so close to the main giant that it appeared to be almost part of it. The stupendous journey across the light years was nearly at an end and the moment was not far distant when Exodus could at last put his plans into action.

There was nothing that he could do now except wait for the electronic brain to give up its control of the switchboard, so he sat down and prepared as best he could to compose himself for that supreme moment.

Silently he reviewed the position to himself, thinking back over the years to the plans he had made before putting himself in the deep sleep.

Yet here was the strange thing. When it came to the time when he ought to remember what it was he ought to do, and in what order he ought to do them, he found himself mentally stumbling. As far as he could recall he must wait for the electronic brain to release the switchboard, then he must switch on the power plant, and then after that he must adjust the controls of the space machine so that.... So that, what?

He put finger and thumb to his eyes and frowned, endeavouring to try and recall the exact scheme that he had in mind, and the trouble was that he had not made any notes, so supremely confident had he been about having everything perfectly clear in his mind.

The cosmic ray generators? Had there been something that he was going to do with them? No, it couldn't have been the generators which came next on the list for he would be able to absorb the necessary cosmic radiation at any time on the journey back to Earth. It did not need to be done now.

What then was it that he had been going to do? He sat scowling, pondering and thinking, until a sudden sharp click and a whirring note made him glance up quickly. The red light on the electronic brain was now glowing with full vigour. At the same moment he beheld the controls on the switchboard jumping and leaping as though controlled by invisible hands.

With a cry of delight he hurried across to them and found each one entirely manageable under his grasp. The machine was free at last for him to do with exactly as he wished.

"This is the moment!" he breathed, his eyes bright. "For a thousand years I have waited for this second. What would you not do now, mother, were you here?"

He reached out his right hand for the main switch of the power plant and drove it home. Immediately the long silent power plant took up the load and then with automatic easy stages began to increase the power with every second. Exodus waited, his eyes on the meters, holding back until the moment when the voltage would be at absolute maximum and he could transfer it to the firing jets of the spaceship.

In between times he glanced out of the window at the colossal blazing bulk of Alpha Centauri and began to wonder anxiously if the voltage would build up quickly enough to enable him to turn the vessel aside in its still hurtling onrush.

If only he could remember what it was he was going to do before starting back on his journey to Earth. He knew that something in the plan had referred to the forward jets of the machine instead of the rear ones and yet....

Yes, of course, that was it! He must use the forward jets before the rear ones so that the recoiling power would thrust him away from Alpha Centauri instead of towards it. If he left the rear ones in full commission his sudden onward surge would force the vessel straight towards that mighty field of gravitation being generated by colossal Alpha.

In that case then it meant a quick reversal in the matter of the switches he was just about to operate. He reached out towards the maze of controls then hesitated again.

For the second time his memory was a complete blank upon which controls he ought to move. This business of memory-slipping was troubling him considerably. He had noticed it quite a deal before descending into the deep sleep and now that he had recovered from it the fault seemed to be even more apparent. Which was the switch that he ought to pull? For the life of him he could not remember!

If it came to that why did he need to return to Earth at all? Looking dazedly out of the window he could see that there were quite a few planets revolving around Alpha at respectable distances, and since many of them had cloud belts he assumed that they had an atmosphere. Whether it was of the type that would suit his form of life he did not know.

Yes, why was he returning to Earth? Here again was the insidious, baffling problem! He had completely forgotten why all this immense expenditure of energy was to be used. The scheme of vengeance upon which he had been engaged for so many years, towards which every one of his energies and mental capabilities had been directed, had vanished from his mind like mist.

He was a man alone in the void and did not know why, was even finding it difficult to realise why he was in the void alone at all.

And being in this condition, with his memory slipping he could not possibly conceive the reason for his peculiar mental blackout. It was in truth the effect of the incessant saturations of cosmic rays that he had absorbed while building his mighty generators for the cause of vengeance.

Far too often had he ignored the immense danger of the position in which he had stood, and instead of mortifying his flesh the cosmic radiations had affected his brain insofar that the powers of memory and remembrance were being totally destroyed.

So Exodus sat at the switchboard, his lower lip beginning to form an imbecilic droop, and his eyes dark pools of wonder as he strove frantically to piece together the missing places in his memory.

He was little more than a scientific god with amnesia. He no longer knew the why or the wherefore. Then a subconscious stirring gave him a brief instant of clarity and he remembered that he had a lever to pull.

He pulled it just at the moment that the atomic power plant reached absolute peak voltage—and that was where he made his mistake. Instead of giving the power to the frontal rockets he had given it to the rear rockets, and with a mighty jolt the space machine suddenly darted off in a direction diagonal to that in which he had been travelling.

This diagonal thrust immediately carried it in the direction of Alpha Centauri and the incredible effulgence of that mighty star blazed through the front window as Exodus turned in horror and closed his eyes against the fiendish glare.

He closed them only for a moment and then jumped to his feet beating his massive fist against the edge of the control board.

"What is it that I have to *remember*? What am I doing *here*? I am here for a purpose but I cannot remember what it is! I have been flung out into this mighty void and I do not know why! What kind of a fool am I that I cannot recall a single iota of the plan which I had in mind...?"

He waited, feeling that perhaps some miracle would grant him sufficient clarity of mind, if only for a moment, to understand the portent of the situation in which he stood. But no such miracle was granted: if anything the obfuscation of his mind deepened even more and became a dark sombre pool in which not a single recollection stirred.

The great control room of the space machine was still filled with that great drowning tide of brilliance. He could feel himself being dragged down to the floor under the incessantly accelerating force of the space machine and the stupendous drag of Alpha itself.

He was forced to his knees. He could only see the mighty bulk of Alpha ahead of him. He had not even the wit nor the sense to realise that the space machine was now irresistibly chained by that stupendous gravitation and no power in the universe could save that great liner from being devoured forever in that liquid hell of flame and fire....

ABOUT THE AUTHOR

British writer **JOHN RUSSELL FEARN** was born near Manchester, England, in 1908. As a child he devoured the science fiction of Wells and Verne, and was a voracious reader of the Boys' Story Papers. He was also fascinated by the cinema, and first broke into print in 1931 with a series of articles in *Film Weekly*.

He then quickly sold his first novel, *The Intelligence Gigantic*, to the American magazine, *Amazing Stories*. Over the next 15 years, writing under several pseudonyms, Fearn became one of the most prolific contributors to all of the leading US science fiction pulps, including such legendary publications as *Astounding Stories*, *Startling Stories*, *Thrilling Wonder Stories*, and *Weird Tales*.

During the late 1940s he diversified into writing novels for the UK market, and also created his famous superwoman character, The Golden Amazon, for the prestigious Canadian magazine, the Toronto *Star Weekly*. In the early 1950s in the UK, his 52 novels as "Vargo Statten" were bestsellers, most notably his novelization of the film, *Creature from the Black Lagoon*.

Apart from science fiction, he had equal success with westerns, romances, and detective fiction, writing an amazing total of 180 novels—most of them in a period of just 10 years—before his early death in 1960. His work has been translated into nine languages, and continues to be reprinted and read worldwide.